SEALED WITH JUSTICE

A CHRISTIAN K9 ROMANTIC SUSPENSE

LAURA SCOTT

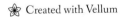

CHAPTER ONE

Kendra Pickett gently massaged her injured shoulder as she walked down the street in her old neighborhood located in Eagle, a suburb to the northeast of Boise, Idaho. The April weather was cool as dusk hovered on the horizon. She was on paid leave from her job as a trauma critical care nurse at a large hospital in Portland, Oregon. The past two years had been rough, first filing for divorce from her husband, then losing her young daughter to cancer. Finding God had been the only thing that had kept her from driving her car into the ocean, and she was grateful for her church friends.

Being forced to stay home had left her at loose ends, and she'd decided a change of scenery was in order. Her dad still lived in Eagle, and visiting with him was no hardship.

Yet coming home brought troubling memories to the surface. Losing her daughter to cancer had been the worst experience of her life, but her divorce from Dr. Don Walker, cheating surgeon extraordinaire, was a welcome relief.

The second worst experience of her life was when Zoey Barkley, her best friend in high school, had gone missing. The seventeen-year-old had been found twelve hours later in a cave on the other side of the creek, strangled to death. Twenty years later, Zoey's murder remained unsolved.

At least, officially, it remained unsolved. Kendra knew Zoey's former boyfriend, Hudson Foster, had killed her, but apparently, the Eagle police didn't have any evidence to prove it. Hudson had claimed he was innocent, but everyone knew he had been in other fights, granted, mostly related to defending his drunken mother.

Even so, there was no denying Hudson had a temper. Plus, he'd left the state to join the military right after graduation. *Running away*, she'd thought sourly. To her knowledge, he hadn't been back since.

It irked her that Hudson had gotten away with killing Zoey. It wasn't right, and while she knew there was no statute of limitations on murder, it wasn't likely that new evidence would come to light now, twenty years later.

Yet that hadn't stopped her from asking questions around town, starting with the police station. So far, her efforts had been met with disdain. Feeling restless, she'd walked from her dad's house down to the river, where she and Zoey had often hung out after school because Zoey hadn't wanted to go home. Zoey's dad had been the Eagle Chief of Police back then, and her brother, Andrew, had bossed Zoey around, making her do all the cooking and cleaning after their mother had passed away. As if those chores were beneath him.

Zoey and Kendra had enjoyed sitting at the creek. They would sit beneath the shelter of large trees, and in the winter, they'd often hide out in the cave.

The same cave where Zoey's body had been found.

Kendra turned off the main road, heading over the hilly

terrain to the creek. Maybe she'd been silly to come here at night, but she wasn't afraid.

Nothing could hurt her anymore, not after she'd lost Olivia. Sweet, sweet Olivia.

Two years felt like another lifetime. She was grateful for the darkness as tears pricked her eyes. Brushing them away, she fought back the memories. She'd cried more in those months after losing Olivia than she had in her entire life.

Tears wouldn't bring Olivia back. Zoey either. They were both with God now, along with her mother, Grace.

Kendra stood for a moment at the water's edge, wishing she could talk to Zoey one last time. Zoey would have been there for her during Olivia's year-long illness. Her friend would have supported her during the divorce too.

"What happened to you, Zoey?" Her voice echoed over the water.

"I've been asking that very same thing," a deep male voice said.

Kendra spun around. She was so badly startled that she tripped over her own feet and hit the ground hard. Then she scrabbled backward to put distance between herself and the man and dog she could barely see standing within the shadows of the trees.

"Who's there?" she asked, squinting through the darkness. So much for thinking she couldn't be scared. Her heart was pounding so fast she thought she'd suffer an acute MI.

"It's me. Hudd and my dog, Echo." A tall, muscular man stepped out from the shadows, a large tan and brown German shepherd at his side. She gaped in surprise at seeing the man she'd just been thinking about.

"When did you get here?" Stupid question, but her brain wasn't firing on all cylinders.

"Here at the creek? Or to Eagle?"

"Both." She rose to her feet and crossed her arms defensively over her chest. Her shoulder hurt worse after hitting the ground, and she gritted her teeth against the pain. Lifting her chin, she stared at him. As a critical care nurse, she'd dealt with her fair share of arrogant surgeons. She'd learned to stand her ground, especially when it came to making sure her patients got the care they needed. Just because Hudson Foster seemed bigger, taller, and stronger than she remembered didn't mean she was going to back down. Although the dog was enough to give her pause. For all she knew, he'd trained the animal to attack humans on command. "You have some nerve asking what happened to Zoey when you're the only one who knows the truth."

"Still beating that drum, huh, Kendra?" He shrugged and glanced off into the distance for a moment before turning back to face her. "I didn't kill her. Had no reason to."

His calm statement caught her off guard. Twenty years ago, he'd seemed desperate for people to believe him. Now, Hudson Foster appeared as if he couldn't care less what people thought.

"Getting angry about Zoey dumping you and attending homecoming with Tristan Donahue is reason enough."

"She tell you that?" Hudd shrugged again, his hand resting on the top of his dog's head. "I was glad she went with Tristan. I had no intention of going to homecoming anyway."

Kendra scowled, wondering if he'd spun this story over the years to cover his tracks. She reached up to massage her left shoulder, praying she hadn't injured it worse. "Whatever. I know the truth."

"You know nothing." For the first time, the hint of anger she remembered from twenty years ago flashed in his eyes.

Then it was gone, and he waved a hand toward the residential area behind them. "Echo and I will walk you home."

"No thanks." The last person she wanted to be seen with was Hudson Foster. She turned and was about to retrace her steps when Hudson unexpectedly emerged beside her, moving with the speed and stealth of a cougar. The dog had also moved without making a sound. She almost fell, but he grabbed her arm, holding her steady.

"We'll walk you home." He said the words as if they were a foregone conclusion.

"I'd rather go alone." She shook off his hand, secretly surprised at his gentle touch. She'd expected brute force from a man with muscles on top of muscles.

Hudson's current physique, even at the age of thirty-nine, made her ex look like a wimp.

And it was different from the way Hudson had looked twenty years ago. Obviously being in the military had changed him. Not that she was remotely interested in a man she knew had murdered her best friend.

"No." Hudson's voice made the hairs on the back of her neck stand up. It was all too familiar to the way Don had treated her at the end of their marriage.

"Yes. Please leave me alone." She took a step away from him at the exact moment a shot rang out.

"Down!" Hudson reacted instinctively, reaching over to pull her down, placing his body over hers while pulling something from his waistband. The dog growled and hovered beside them. With her face plastered against the ground, she couldn't tell what was going on, until she heard more gunfire. Much louder.

Coming from Hudson? Was he armed too?

What on earth had she gotten herself into?

SURPRISINGLY, the gunfire had come from the direction of the residential neighborhood. Hudd couldn't pinpoint an exact location, although he did his best to sweep his good eye over the area.

After he'd returned fire, he thought he'd heard a car engine, possibly the gunman leaving the scene. His hearing was more acute now that he'd lost the vision in his left eye. Their last SEAL op had gone sideways, and he'd been hit in the eye with a piece of debris. Thankfully, his right eye had been spared, and he wasn't completely blind.

"Easy, Echo." The dog calmed but still looked alert. Hudd stayed exactly where he was, covering Kendra's slim body with his, refusing to assume they were safe. If he'd been the gunman, he'd have taken cover and waited for them to stand up before trying again.

Not that Hudson would have missed the first time. He'd been one of the better marksmen of their team, second only to Dallas.

After several long moments, Kendra pushed at him. "Let me up. I can't breathe!"

He knew his weight could be crushing her, so he shifted to the side but didn't let up. "Stay down. I don't know if the shooter is still out there."

"You're the shooter," she accused. "I heard your gun go off."

"In self-defense." He was getting mighty tired of defending himself. Kendra had made it clear she thought he was guilty of killing Zoey, and normally that wouldn't matter.

Except for some reason, it did. Especially coming from Kendra, a girl he'd secretly crushed on back in high school.

Only Kendra had dated Corey Robinson, the quarter-back of the football team.

Whatever. What did that matter? No reason to dwell on stuff that happened twenty years ago. He continued scanning the area, searching for any sign of the gunman. Finally, he stood and offered a hand to Kendra. To his surprise, she took it. He pulled her to her feet, then quickly released her. He didn't holster his weapon, preferring to keep it in hand. "Heel, Echo."

The dog came to sit at his side.

"I don't understand what happened," she said with a frown. "Is someone trying to kill you?"

"I'm not sure if I was the target or you were." He thought back to those last seconds before hearing the gunshot. "You moved away from me, remember? I think the bullet passed between us."

"Me?" Kendra's jaw dropped. "That's impossible. I've only been here two days, why would someone shoot at me?"

"I don't know." Hudd didn't like the situation one bit. He'd been in Eagle for almost a week, minus two days of traveling to Los Angeles and back, but he'd made sure not to be seen around town.

To be honest, he wasn't sure why he'd announced his presence to Kendra. If he had stayed silent, she'd have never seen him and Echo.

Although if he hadn't shown himself, she might already be dead.

He grimaced. This was why you didn't play the what-if game. Better to focus on the situation as is. No point in trying to change the past.

"This way." He pulled her toward the trees where he'd been crouched when she'd arrived at the creek. Echo came with him, staying close to his left side. It was his vulnerable side after he'd lost vision in that eye. He focused on Kendra. "Are you sure there isn't anyone after you? A boyfriend, husband, or jilted lover?"

She stared up at him. "My ex-husband left me for another woman, no reason for him to come after me. Besides, he's in Portland, Oregon."

"And no other men in your life?" Why he was pressing he had no clue.

She shook her head. "No. And I don't see why anyone would shoot at me. I think you must be the target. The guy missed because he's probably just a lousy shot and couldn't see clear in the darkness."

"Motive?" Hudson drawled.

"I'm sure you've made enemies over the years." She waved a hand. "And showing up here after all this time is just asking for trouble. The entire town believes you killed Zoey twenty years ago; my guess is that someone is trying to make you pay for that."

"Like Zoey's brother, Andrew, or her father? George retired from his job as police chief two years ago but still actively hunts, and Andrew is the new chief of police. I doubt either one of them would have missed me."

Kendra opened her mouth, then closed it again. Then she shivered, and he had the ridiculous urge to wrap his arm around her. It almost made him smile to imagine her punching him in the stomach or slapping his face in response.

Almost.

Hudd hadn't smiled or laughed in the months since being medically discharged from the navy minus one eye while suffering terrible migraine headaches. If not for Echo, he figured he'd be dead by now.

"We can't just hide here." Kendra sounded annoyed. "I need to get home. My dad will wonder where I am."

He already knew Kendra had come home for a few weeks and was staying with her father at the house she grew up in. He'd kept his ears open while staying out of sight. It was surprising what the good citizens of Eagle discussed when they didn't know anyone was listening.

But now wasn't the time to tell her everything he knew. Including the murmurings of why people were asking about a twenty-year-old cold case.

"I need you to stay here while I check out the area to make sure the gunman isn't still hiding nearby." He stared down at her and mustered all the politeness he could find. "Kendra, will you please stay here for me? I really don't want anything to happen to you."

"Again, you're assuming the gunman was after me." Her tone lacked conviction as if she might be realizing the second possibility wasn't something to brush off so easily. "Yes, I'll wait here."

"Thank you." He gently positioned her up against the thickest tree trunk. "Stay right here until I return. Echo, guard." The dog sat, his large ears perked forward. "Good boy."

"Oh, for Pete's sake . . . hey, where did you go?" The last words were said in a hushed whisper.

Hudd didn't answer as he'd already left the clearing beneath the trees to move over the rocky, hilly terrain. The sound of water rushing through the creek helped cover the sound of his footsteps. Despite his large size, his SEAL training had taught him how to move silently, blending in with the environment.

Every few steps he paused to listen. He didn't hear anything other than the muted traffic and the occasional door slamming from the residential neighborhood beyond the hill. It was a far cry from the abandoned shack he'd grown up in on the outskirts of town.

It didn't take him long to clear the area. When he was satisfied the gunman was gone, he returned to Kendra and Echo.

"I never heard you!" Her tone carried a hint of accusation. "How did you do that?"

"Training." He gave Echo the hand signal to come, and the dog trotted over. "The area is clear. Are you ready to go?"

"Yes." He was glad Kendra didn't bother to argue about his plan to escort her home. The gunshot had obviously shaken her. And with good reason.

The more he thought about it, the more he was convinced Kendra was the gunman's intended target. "Might be better for you to head back to Portland."

"What?" She frowned at him. "Why would I do that?"

"To be safe." He hesitated, then asked, "Have you been asking questions about Zoey's murder since you've been home?"

Her eyes narrowed. "Did you hear that from someone in particular?"

He didn't respond.

After a full minute, she sighed. "Yes, I went to the Eagle police station to ask if they'd solved her murder. I was able to speak to Roger, one of the officers on duty, who told me the case was still open, but no one was actively pursuing it."

That much he'd gathered for himself based on the rudimentary internet search he'd done and the bits of conversations he'd overheard. Still, he remained silent, waiting for her to continue.

"I may have suggested that I planned to check out our

old hangouts to see if I could find out anything." She waved a hand. "But that was mostly just talk on my part. I didn't really think I'd be able to find anything. Besides, even if I did, who would care? Unless—wait a minute, you can't seriously think the killer is still living here."

"Why not?"

"I don't know." She sounded exasperated. "Most people don't stick around Eagle forever. They move closer to Boise or out of state."

"We did, yes. But not everyone. Zoey's family is still here and so are a few of our former classmates." Hudd frowned, thinking about what she'd said. "I heard that someone was asking questions about Zoey's murder, but I didn't realize you were the source."

She kicked at a rock. "Seems to me the Eagle police department should have continued to investigate. I can't imagine there's a ton of crimes keeping them busy."

He felt compelled to agree with her on that front. Eagle had never been a hotbed of crime, outside of the usual drugs, alcohol abuse, petty theft kind of thing. Zoey's murder had been huge, and Police Chief George Barkley had sworn to bring the perpetrator to justice.

Only he never had.

Not that the guy hadn't tried everything possible to convince Hudson to confess to the crime. The chief had kept Hudson in the box for hours on end, forcing him to repeat his story over and over. Until Hudson wised up and asked for a lawyer.

Still, Barkley had kept him in jail overnight claiming it was too late to get a lawyer. By the morning, though, the police had reluctantly let him go.

The only alibi he had at the time was his mother who'd been drunk as usual. Which wouldn't have held up in a court of law if there had been any other evidence to tie him to the crime.

Thankfully, there wasn't.

Hudd knew that was because he didn't kill Zoey. Although he'd kept expecting to get arrested again, despite the lack of evidence. And after he'd finally graduated from high school, he'd gone to the Boise armed services office and signed up to join the navy. He'd told the recruiter that he wanted to be a Navy SEAL, and the guy had smiled and nodded.

That's a fine goal, son, but you gotta understand only the toughest men of the bunch get through BUD/S training.

The recruiter had been right about that. Getting through BUD/S training had been the hardest thing he'd ever done. Kaleb was his swim buddy, the two of them leaning on each other to get through the program.

Hudd had given twenty years of his life to the navy. Unlike Kaleb, he hadn't tried to sustain a marriage throughout his deployments overseas. Being alone had suited him just fine. He didn't regret the path he'd chosen except maybe that last op that had claimed the life of their teammate, Jaydon Rampart.

"If you didn't kill Zoey, then who did?" Kendra's question broke into his thoughts.

"Beats me." He didn't bother to reiterate his innocence. "I've often wondered if it wasn't one of the football players. Maybe one of the guys who wanted Zoey but couldn't have her."

"Come on, really? I can't believe you're accusing my old boyfriend or one of his close friends of killing Zoey. That's ridiculous."

"Is it?" He'd personally never cared for any of the guys,

they'd always acted as if they were better than everyone else.

Especially him.

Coach Donahue had tried to convince him to play, as he could run fast, but Hudd had declined. Not just because of the way the other guys treated him but because he had to work two jobs after school. Heaven knew his mother couldn't hold a job.

"I know they weren't always nice to you, Hudson," she admitted. "But they weren't bad guys. Just a little too cocky for their own good."

That was putting it mildly. "And they were also the least likely to be considered a serious suspect by Chief Barkley as his son was part of the group. They were all at some party from what I remember."

She didn't have a quick response to that, and they walked in silence for a few moments. Then she asked, "Where are you staying?"

"Does it matter?"

She stopped and turned to look at him. They were in the residential neighborhood now, and the streetlights illuminated her features. He had to admit, Kendra was even more beautiful than she had been twenty years ago. Her blond hair wasn't as long, she wore it in a chin-length bob, but the style suited her. Her dark eyes seemed to draw him into their depths. "I'm just making polite conversation. Are you always so prickly?"

"Yeah." He glanced at Echo who was looking up at him as if trying to figure out what was going on. "I'm staying at the shack out in the woods. Believe it or not, it's still there even though my mom passed away ten years ago."

"Your old house? But it's . . ." Her voice trailed off.

"Barely standing? Doesn't have electricity or running

water? I know, but it's not as bad as some places I've stayed in." He'd take the old shack over the desert of Afghanistan any day.

"But—why? Do you need money? I can loan you some."

The rusty croaking sound coming from his throat was laughter. It surprised him more than it did her. "No, I have money."

Kendra was staring at him oddly, not unlike Echo, then she shook her head and shrugged. He could tell she was thinking he had more than a few screws loose in the old noggin.

And maybe he did.

"How long are you staying?" she asked.

It was a good question. One of the many reasons he'd gone to the old shack rather than getting a motel room was that he preferred to come and go as he pleased. Especially important when a bad migraine hit.

He wasn't sure why he'd come back to Eagle in the first place. To face the memories of his mother? To prove to Barkley that he'd made something of himself?

To clear his name?

None of that really mattered. He could have easily left town early the next morning without anyone even realizing he was there.

It occurred to him that whoever had taken that shot at Kendra may have caught a glimpse of his face. If so, there was no reason to skulk around.

And more reason for him to stay, especially if Kendra was in danger.

"Hudson?" Kendra prodded.

"Three weeks." He glanced at her. "That's how long you're planning to stay, right?"

She looked taken aback. "Why does that matter?"

"You poked the sleeping bear, Kendra. You asked questions about Zoey's murder and made it clear you were going to search for answers." He wanted to shake some sense into her. "Haven't you figured out yet that you're in danger? The gunfire was intentional. I'm staying until I can figure out what is going on."

She gaped at him, then shivered again. As if on cue, bright headlights came out of the darkness, heading straight toward them. "Go, Echo!" Thankfully, the dog lurched to the side. Hudson grabbed Kendra, swinging her out of harm's way just as the edge of the car's bumper clipped his left knee, sending pain zinging through him. He managed to stay on his feet, but just barely.

His stupid peripheral vision sucked, or he could have avoided the car altogether. Unfortunately, by the time he spun around to find the vehicle responsible, the taillights were gone.

Two attempts to hurt or kill Kendra in less than two hours?

Not good.

CHAPTER TWO

Somehow, Kendra managed to stay on her feet after Hudson swung her out of the way of the car. She was stunned at the realization he was right about someone trying to hurt her.

If not for Hudson's lightning-fast reflexes, she'd be lying on the ground right now.

"Are you okay?" Hudson's tense tone had her dragging her gaze to his. Echo had returned to his side. He rested his hand on the shepherd's head as if to reassure him. She found it a bit odd that the dog rarely barked and wondered if that was the way Hudson had trained him. "You're holding your shoulder, did I hurt you?"

"I—had surgery on my shoulder about four weeks ago." She dropped her hand. Granted, he had grabbed her arm, which had put pressure on the tender joint, but her injuries could have been so much worse.

He winced. "I didn't realize."

"How could you? Besides, knowing wouldn't have changed anything. You yanked me out of the way to save my life." She shivered, and he stepped closer. "I guess you were right about me poking the sleeping bear."

He didn't gloat or point out how silly she'd been to think otherwise. "Yeah. You should call the police."

"And tell them what? That a bullet whizzed past me and a car nearly ran me off the road, but I have no idea who might be responsible?"

"Exactly. At least get the attempts on record."

She shook her head, feeling as if doing such a thing would be useless. She could just imagine the look on Officer Roger's face. "I'll think about it."

There was a pause before Hudson said, "Okay, then let's get you home."

As they continued walking, she couldn't help but glance constantly over her shoulder. "Do you think I'll be safe at my dad's house?"

"I hope so." His response wasn't exactly reassuring. "What happened to your shoulder?"

"I was lifting a heavy patient, and the nurse helping me tripped over a cord and let go of her side. I tore my rotator cuff."

"You're a nurse?"

"Yes. I work in the Trauma Surgical Intensive Care Unit in Portland's largest hospital."

"Impressive. I have a lot of respect for nurses."

His comment surprised her and not just because he apparently had firsthand knowledge of being cared for by a nurse. Hudson seemed so different now than he had been twenty years ago. Then again, she'd grown and changed too. Still, she didn't think a person's basic personality changed that much.

Had she misjudged him twenty years ago? Her cheeks burned with embarrassment remembering how she'd accused him of killing Zoey. Back when they'd first found Zoey's body and again tonight.

"I'm sorry. I never should have accused you of killing Zoey."

He nodded but remained silent.

"What branch of service did you join?" She had no idea why she was making small talk, other than it was a good way to ignore the fact that someone had just tried to kill her, twice.

"Navy."

She eyed his large physique. "Really? I'd have taken you for some sort of Green Beret or Army Ranger. I can't see you wearing a sailor's cap."

The corner of his mouth quirked in what might have been a pathetic attempt at a smile. "I was a Navy SEAL."

Of course, he was. "That's more impressive than being a nurse."

"No. You save people's lives. That's very important."

She was pretty sure he'd saved lives by getting rid of the enemy, but it was obvious he didn't really care to talk about it. "You're still a SEAL?"

"Retired."

She wanted to ask more, but her father's house was up ahead. Kendra really hoped she wasn't putting her father in danger by staying there. Should she head over to the motel?

"Echo, stay."

The dog dropped into a sitting position, looking up at Hudson as if waiting for his next command. She didn't have personal experience with dogs, her mother had been allergic, but this one was extremely well trained.

"Thanks for walking me home." She tried to smile. "Be careful heading back to the shack. There's still a possibility you're the target."

"I'll stick around here, make sure no one bothers you."

"What?" She frowned. "You can't do that. It's freezing out."

He held her gaze. "Good night, Kendra."

She looked from Hudson to her father's house and back. Somehow, she just knew that Hudson would in fact stay outside all night to watch over her. To be fair, it probably wasn't that much different from sleeping in the shack he'd grown up in. The place didn't have any heat, although it did have an old wood-burning stove. Unless someone had ripped it off.

Either way, it didn't matter. She'd never be able to sleep knowing he was out there. "Do you want to sleep on the sofa? My dad is probably already in bed. He tends to go to bed early because he gets up at the crack of dawn to go to work."

"Does he still work at the power plant?"

"Yes." She was impressed he'd remembered. "Echo is welcome too."

He hesitated, then finally nodded. "Okay."

"Thanks." She couldn't help feeling relieved. "Dad may have some questions for you in the morning."

"I'll leave before he wakes up to find me here." Hudson glanced at Echo. "Give me a minute to walk him around the block. That way he'll know it's time to do his business."

"Ah, okay." She used her key to unlock the front door. Once inside, she quickly confirmed her father was indeed in his room with the door shut. She grabbed a pillow and blanket out of the hallway closet and carried them to the sofa. It was a normal size but probably still too short for Hudson.

When she saw him approach the front door, she hurried

over to let him in, gesturing toward the living room. "The sofa is a bit short," she said apologetically.

"It's fine. Thanks." He didn't look concerned. It made her wonder what he was sleeping on in the shack. Was there furniture in the place? Or was he sleeping on the floor?

Not her problem. Now that she could see him clearly with the living room lamp on, she noticed he had a left eye prosthesis, along with a small white scar along the corner of that same eye. Apparently, something had gone wrong during one of his SEAL missions. Was that why he'd mentioned having respect for nurses? The fact that he hadn't mentioned his disability and that he hadn't let it stop him from shielding her with his own body when danger was near was humbling. The man had more integrity in his pinkie finger than Don had in his whole body. Something she should have figured out sooner rather than later.

With an effort, she put her past mistakes behind her. "Um, the bathroom is down the hall. Don't worry about waking my dad, he sleeps like a rock."

"Thanks."

"Let me know if you need anything." She was starting to babble now and tried her best to stop. "Good night, Hudson."

"Good night."

His husky voice sent tingles down her spine. Kendra mentally rolled her eyes at her foolishness as she went to her room. Ridiculous to put Hudson on some sort of pedestal. Hadn't she been impressed with Don's skill as a doctor when they'd first met? He'd only been a resident at the time, but even then, he'd had a great bedside manner with his patients.

Kendra had married him, supported him financially and

emotionally throughout his five-year residency program, until he'd become a full-fledged trauma surgeon.

That was when he'd grown arrogant, especially when they were at work. At first, she thought it was his way of not giving her special treatment, but when he reamed her out one day in front of a patient's family, she'd confronted him. He'd had the nerve to laugh it off as if it didn't matter.

Then she found out she was pregnant. So she'd done her best to make things work.

Until she realized his bedside manner had included bedding her fellow nursing colleagues, women far younger than her. She'd kicked him out six weeks before Olivia was diagnosed with cancer. They'd come together, for the sake of their daughter, but Olivia had died before her fifth birthday.

And the night Olivia had gone home to God, Don was supposedly on call. Only the truth was that he was staying overnight with his new woman.

She punched the pillow and sighed. There was no reason to compare Don to Hudson. They were as different as night and day. One man who'd used his hands to save trauma victims' lives, the other who'd used his hands to fire a weapon in defense of his country.

Kendra tossed and turned, unable to stop her racing thoughts. It seemed clear that Hudson hadn't killed Zoey. After the way he'd saved her life twice tonight, it was impossible to imagine him choking her best friend.

Was he right about the real killer being one of the football players? Anything was possible. But maybe Zoey's killer wasn't a fellow student at all. There were too many possible suspects to count. Which was why everyone had focused on Hudson Foster, Zoey's former boyfriend and son of the town drunk.

What bothered her more was that the killer must still be living in the area. Otherwise, why come after her? She grimaced as she stared up at the ceiling.

She never should have opened her big fat mouth.

Kendra must have slept at some point because she blinked in the darkness when she heard the sound of a door closing. Instantly wide awake, she threw off the covers and ran her fingers through her tangled hair as she headed out to check on Hudson.

The man and his dog were gone. Not only that, but the pillow and blanket had been returned to the linen closet, the living room appearing as if the pair had never been there at all.

She blew out a breath, ignoring the stab of disappointment. Hudson had said he'd leave early, before her dad woke up.

Apparently, the guy meant what he said. A trait she should have appreciated twenty years ago when he'd claimed he was innocent of killing Zoey.

"Kendra? What are you doing up so early?" She turned to see her dad standing in the hallway. "Your shoulder bothering you?"

"A little." She managed a smile. "Would you like me to make breakfast before you head out?"

"Nah, you know I like to stop and have my usual breakfast sandwich on the way to work." It was a bad habit her dad had fallen into since her mother had passed away. She'd tried to convince him the fast-food sandwiches weren't healthy, but he didn't care. "Don't trouble yourself. Go back to bed, get some sleep."

"Okay." She padded back to her room, knowing getting more sleep was impossible. Now that she was up, her shoulder ached worse than ever. Hitting the ground twice yesterday hadn't helped. After taking a shower, she sat down to do the exercise routine recommended by her physical therapist.

Yet her mind wandered as she went through the various stretches and movements. Maybe Hudson was right about reporting the incidents to the police. It couldn't hurt to have the attempts on record.

But then what? She'd started the whole thing by poking her nose into Zoey's murder. Silly, really, as she was a critical care nurse, not a detective.

For a nanosecond, she considered packing her suitcase and heading back to Portland. Then she stiffened her resolve. No way. What if the killer followed her there to finish the job?

Running wasn't the answer. Getting to the truth was the only way she'd really be safe.

And for that, she'd need Hudson's help.

HUDD HADN'T SLEPT GREAT, despite the cushy sofa that was a hundred times more comfortable than sleeping on the floor in the shack. His goal had been to listen for any sign the gunman had returned. Deep down, he'd also been afraid of suffering a wicked migraine headache, which was normally accompanied by nightmares of their last op.

Thankfully, he hadn't suffered either phenomenon. Hudd figured he'd gotten almost four hours of sleep, which wasn't bad. The moment he'd heard movement coming from Kendra's father's room, he'd bolted upright, folded the blanket, and tucked it with the pillow in the linen closet. He and Echo slipped out the front door before her father knew he'd been there.

As he walked back to the shack, he glanced at Echo. The dog had slept well, maybe because of the warmth of the cozy house rather than being in the shack.

Now that at least two people, Kendra and the shooter, knew he was in town, Hudd realized he should probably check out the closest motel. If there was one that allowed dogs.

The shack was isolated from town, which wouldn't be helpful if the gunman made another attempt to harm Kendra. He needed to figure out a way to convince her to head back to Portland.

As soon as possible.

When he headed down the dirt road leading to his childhood home, he slowed his pace, listening intently. He was armed with his 9mm Sig Sauer, and his MK 3 knife, both preferred weapons of the SEAL teams. He raked his good eye over the terrain, searching for any sign of an intruder. Two-legged or four, although he was far more apprehensive about the two-legged variety.

In his experience, man was more lethal than beast.

To his surprise, he didn't find anything amiss. He entered the shack, ignoring the musty dilapidated sight, and quickly fed Echo. Then he went around to the side of the structure to examine his Jeep. That, too, appeared untouched.

It didn't take him long to pack up his things. He didn't have much, and what mattered was the dog dishes, food, and toys for Echo.

He'd been training the German shepherd ever since he'd been discharged from the hospital. He and the rest of his teammates had all been given dogs by Lillian, the woman who dedicated her life to rescuing animals. They'd named their dogs after the Greek alphabet used by the navy. Echo responded extremely well to his commands and probably would have made an awesome police dog.

Hudson was thankful to have Echo with him. He'd gone off-grid, feeling like a wounded animal needing time and space to lick his wounds. Being around his teammates had been difficult. But that wasn't the case with Echo.

The dog was a great companion. Every time he awoke from a night terror, Echo was there, licking his face or nudging him with his nose. When he couldn't get up due to the debilitating migraines, Echo stayed right by his side, crowding close as if to offer comfort.

"You're a good boy," he murmured, scratching the dog behind his ears.

Those large ears flickered a few seconds before Hudson heard the rumble of a car engine. Without hesitation, he went into hunter mode, pulling his weapon from its holster and sliding to the side of the door. He gave Echo the hand signal to stay.

In the distance, he caught a hint of movement through the bare trees, which were just beginning to show signs of springtime buds. He swiftly considered his options.

Wait there and confront the intruder at gunpoint or head out the back with Echo, disappearing from sight. The latter would mean leaving his Jeep, and he didn't much care for that plan. Especially since Echo's things were packed inside.

He waited, frowning when a small bright red sedan bounced into view. It took a moment to recognize Kendra was behind the wheel.

Why had she come here? He grimaced, realizing he shouldn't have told her where he was staying. Yet, deep down, he was happy to see her. Which only proved he had several screws loose in the old brain.

He holstered his gun and opened the warped door. He stepped out onto the sagging porch to wait for her.

"Hey." She smiled as she slid out from behind the wheel.

"What are you doing here?" His question sounded harsher than he intended. He blamed it on the fact that he wasn't used to talking this much.

"I—was hoping you would come with me to the police department." He kicked himself for the flash of hurt in her brown eyes.

"Sorry, I didn't mean to sound gruff." He tried to smile. "Haven't had any coffee yet."

"Oh, I picked some up on the way!" She immediately brightened and rounded the front of the vehicle to the passenger side. She pulled out a to-go container with two coffee cups. "I wasn't sure how you liked it, so I brought extra creamers and sugars."

"I—thanks." He couldn't remember the last time anyone had done something so simple as to buy him coffee. He walked forward to take the container from her hands. "I drink mine black."

"Me too." Her smile widened. "Cream and sugar ruins the taste."

His preference had been born out of necessity; black coffee was all you could get while being deployed overseas. "I'd offer for you to come in, but there isn't anywhere to sit."

"Have you been sleeping on the floor?" She looked appalled. "That can't be comfortable."

He almost pointed out that life was never easy but managed to hold his tongue. The SEAL mantra was that the only easy day was yesterday. They stood awkwardly, sipping from their coffees, until Kendra gestured toward her cheery red car. "We can sit inside, where it's warmer."

He immediately glanced at Echo. "Let's go to my Jeep. There's a crate area for Echo in the back."

"You have a Jeep?"

He wasn't sure why she was so shocked. Then again, he supposed she was still thinking he was some poor homeless guy without any money to stay at a motel. "Come, Echo." He turned and used the key fob in his pocket to unlock the doors. He opened the passenger door for Kendra, then put Echo in the back. He sat in the driver's seat and glanced at her. "I'm not broke."

"Sorry." Her cheeks went pink. "It's just difficult for me to understand why you would choose to stay here."

He didn't have a good answer for that, so he sipped his coffee.

"I really would like you to come to the police station with me." She turned in her seat to face him. "You're a witness to both attempts, Hudson. Besides, this should help back up your story that you didn't kill Zoey."

He scowled. "Maybe."

"It will! And if I'm being totally honest, I would like your support." She hesitated, then added, "I know I don't deserve it after the way I treated you."

"Don't worry about it. I've had worse insults hurtled at me." He managed another smile. "Some of my COs could really lay it on thick."

"CO?"

"Commanding Officer." He took another sip of his coffee. "I'll gladly go with you to the police station, Kendra. I doubt they can arrest me after all these years."

Her jaw dropped. "I hadn't thought of that! Is that why you're staying way out here? So no one knows you're back in town?"

He nodded. "Figure the cat is out of the bag now."

She chewed her lower lip in a way that made him think of kissing her to make her stop. "I don't know, Hudson. It's not good that Andrew Barkley is the current chief of police. What if he does decide to have his cops toss you in jail?"

He was touched by her concern for his welfare. "They won't. Besides, as you said, we were together when the shooting happened and when the car tried to run you off the road."

"I guess." She frowned. "But I don't know who we can trust. I couldn't sleep last night, going through all the possible suspects. Not just students, but adults too. Like Mark, the grocery store manager who Zoey often complained about. He was always leering at the pretty girls, making them uncomfortable. And what if the killer isn't a man but a woman? Maybe Zoey was killed out of jealousy?"

"There are a lot of possible suspects that were never seriously considered," Hudd agreed.

"Yeah, because everyone just assumed it was you." She huffed in disgust. "If they'd tried harder to consider other suspects, they may have found the real culprit."

Those were the exact words he'd tossed at George Barkley twenty years ago. But the chief of police had sneered at him that they already had the right guy, and that was Hudson.

It was then that he'd known it was time to get out of town before someone got desperate enough to frame him for the murder.

Even though that meant leaving his mother behind.

Oh, he'd tried to convince her to move to San Diego to be near the naval base. She'd flat-out refused. And then she'd gotten drunk and passed out.

Over the years, Hudd had sent her money each month to help support her. Until she'd died. Then he'd paid to have her buried in the cemetery where his grandparents had been laid to rest.

He hadn't come back, until now.

He downed the rest of his coffee and started the Jeep. "Let's do this."

"I can drive," she protested.

He ignored her. "We're already here, and it's better for Echo."

She nodded, clicking her seat belt into place. The drive to the police station didn't take long. Hudd wasn't surprised to note the place hadn't changed much in the years he'd been gone. He left the windows open for Echo, although he could also remotely start the car to provide heat for his companion if needed.

As they walked up the steps to the front door, the back of his neck tingled. He stopped and turned toward his blind side, then locked gazes with his former nemesis, Andrew Barkley. Hudd easily recognized him, despite the balding hair and paunchy gut.

It was clear in Andrew's icy gaze that he recognized Hudd too. The sheer hatred in the current police chief's eyes told him everything he needed to know.

Hudd might have come home, but he wasn't welcome.

Forcing him to admit it was very possible he was the intended target of the gunfire and the near-miss crash after all.

CHAPTER THREE

When Hudson's body tensed, Kendra followed his gaze to Andrew Barkley. Seeing the glimmer of hate reflected in the chief's eyes concerned her.

She grabbed Hudson's arm. "Let's go, no reason to do this."

"No." Hudson's one-word responses were driving her batty. Had he always been like that? To her shame, she hadn't bothered to talk to him much twenty years ago.

Fine. She quickly changed her plan. "Andrew!" She smiled and waved. "It's great to see you again! So nice to hear you followed in your father's footsteps."

"Kendra, I heard you'd come home for a few weeks." Andrew's smile didn't reach his narrow eyes. "I find it interesting you're so chummy with Foster after what happened to my sister and your best friend."

"Oh, well, you wouldn't believe what we've been through!" Kendra continued as if she hadn't noticed the animosity seething between the two men. "We were at the creek, and someone fired a gun at us! Then when Hudson was walking me home, a car tried to run us off the road!" She kept her gaze on Andrew, gauging his reaction.

"Oh yeah?" The police chief's expression was full of doubt. "Were there any witnesses? Did you call the police?"

"That's why we're here now, to file a police report." She couldn't tell what Andrew was thinking.

"We'd both like to provide our statements," Hudson said, breaking his silence. "These events need to be on record in case something happens again."

For a moment, it looked as if Andrew might snap at Hudson, but then he turned away. "Fine with me. The officer at the front desk will take your complaint."

Once Andrew was gone, she glanced up at Hudson. "That wasn't nice. I feel terrible dragging you down here."

"Don't. I'm fine." Hudson rested his hand in the small of her back. "Let's do this."

The warmth of his hand made it difficult to concentrate. This weird awareness of Hudson had to stop. Neither one of them would be in Eagle for long before they went back to their respective lives.

Yet, deep down, she could admit how she'd never felt this way with Don. She'd admired him as a resident, a guy who actually listened to the nurse's opinion. And she'd been impressed by his skill. He'd been sweet when they'd first gotten married and grateful for her help in supporting him through those difficult residency years.

Then his ego had gotten blown way out of proportion, turning him into someone she didn't recognize. Easy to see now she was better off without him. And maybe this odd response to Hudson was a reaction to being alone for so long. Dating hadn't interested her in the least after losing Olivia.

Why was she thinking about it now?

Hudson opened the door for her. They entered the police station and walked up to the counter. She'd expected the officer there to be aware of why they were there, but clearly Andrew hadn't bothered to say anything.

Officer Aaron Campbell agreed to take their statements. He seemed earnest enough, expressing concern over gunfire happening in their small town.

"You should interview the residents living along the creek," Hudson said. "They'll have heard something."

"Oh yes, of course," Campbell agreed.

From the corner of Kendra's eye, she could see Andrew standing off to the side, speaking to one of his officers. They were smiling and laughing as if a serious crime hadn't just happened under their nose.

In that moment, Andrew reminded her very much of Don. Full of himself and unwilling to be bothered by the small stuff.

Not that gunfire and being run off the road should be considered minor crimes. Just the opposite.

After they left the police station, Hudson gestured toward the Corner Café. "Breakfast?"

"Sure." She'd had a bowl of oatmeal earlier but doubted there was any food in the shack where Hudson had stayed. And she wasn't ready to end her time with him either.

"I need to check on Echo first." Hudson went over to the Jeep and opened the back. Echo jumped down, wagging his tail with excitement.

"I hate the thought of him being stuck in the car," she said. "Bring him along."

He raised a brow. "Dogs aren't allowed in restaurants."

"They are if they're service dogs. Trust me, we see service dogs in the hospital all the time. If you tell them he's a service dog, they can't kick him out unless, of course, he lunges at someone or tries to bite the staff."

"He won't." Hudson reached into the back of the Jeep and pulled out a leash. "You really have service dogs in the hospital?"

"All the time." She grinned. "I was the charge nurse one day and had to kick one lady's dog out when the little yappy thing bit a nurse's finger. You should have seen that woman, ripping the EKG wires off her chest, crying out in a dramatic way that if her dog had to go, then she was going too."

The corner of Hudson's mouth tipped up in a smile. "Did you let her go?"

"Yep." She fell into step beside him. "True service dogs don't bite."

"Echo would never do that unless, of course, I told him to attack."

She eyed the large shepherd. "I'd back off if I saw Echo coming after me."

"Exactly."

The restaurant was more than half full. Kendra could feel dozens of curious gazes watching as the hostess escorted them to a booth in the corner. She figured the entire town would know she'd had breakfast with Hudson Foster before noon.

"Down," Hudson told Echo. Obediently, the dog stretched out on the floor beneath the table.

Their server, who looked all of twenty years old, brought two waters and poured coffee. "My name is Jeanie, do you need a few minutes or are you ready to order?"

"Ah, a few minutes, please." Kendra glanced at Hudson who simply nodded.

"Okay, take your time." Jeanie hurried off.

"Lots of new faces around town."

Hudson raised a brow. "We are twenty years older. I'm sure the town has changed more than it has stayed the same."

"I know." She tried to focus on the menu, but she was still troubled by Andrew Barkley's attitude. She leaned forward and lowered her voice. "We really need to figure out who killed Zoey. That will clear your name once and for all."

"Kendra." He said her name on a sigh. "The only thing you're going to do is drive back to Portland."

She shook her head but didn't want to argue about it here. Not when they were already drawing all kinds of attention. Maybe having breakfast at the most popular café in town wasn't the best idea in the world.

After they placed their orders, yogurt parfait for her and a meat-lovers omelet for Hudson, she sipped her coffee and stared out the window at the town she once called home. Strange, really, that she'd always thought this was the perfect place to grow up. That being outside of the big city covered them with a safety net.

Zoey's murder had changed that, and more.

"Evil can lurk anywhere," Hudson said, reading her thoughts.

"I know." Working trauma had shown her what people were capable of, shooting each other with guns, stabbing with knives. She'd even cared for some horrific physical assault victims who were beaten within an inch of their life. "I've seen it more than I care to."

Hudson frowned. "As a nurse?"

"Yes." She grimaced. "I work trauma, remember? Lots of victims of violence."

"I can imagine." He looked upset at this news, and for

some reason, that made her want to hug him. "You've become quite an amazing woman, Kendra."

"And you're a great guy." She had to force herself to look away, lest she drown in his large blue gaze. "We'll need to discuss our next steps."

His frown deepened. "*We* aren't taking any."

Oh yes, they were. But she didn't speak her thoughts out loud because Jeanie arrived with their meals. Kendra clasped her hands in her lap, bowed her head, and silently thanked God for their food and asked that He continue to protect them as they searched for the truth.

When she finished, she found Hudson watching her curiously. "What? You never saw anyone pray before eating a meal?"

"My swim buddy, Kaleb, prays often." Hudson reached for his fork. "I just didn't expect you to do the same."

"I lost my daughter, Olivia, to cancer two years ago." The words tumbled out before she could stop them. "I was so angry after she was diagnosed, but the hospital chaplain visited with me every day. I'd seen him do that in the ICU, of course, but being on the other end was—humbling to say the least."

"I'm so sorry, Kendra."

Hudson's sympathy almost brought a fresh spurt of tears. She did her best to hold them back. "Thanks. Anyway, it was the most difficult thing I'd been through, and in hindsight, I wouldn't have survived without the chaplain's support."

"What about your ex-husband?"

She let out a harsh laugh. "Don was too busy sleeping with his latest girlfriend to answer my call about Olivia taking a turn for the worst. She died before he showed up reeking of the woman's perfume."

"Jerk."

"Yep." She took a bite of her yogurt topped with blueberries and strawberries. "Enough about me. We all have been through difficulties in our lives. I know you've been through a rough time too."

He paused with his fork halfway to his mouth. Then he nodded slowly. "As a nurse, I'm sure it's easy for you to tell I lost my left eye."

"You've adapted extremely well," she said. "I honestly didn't notice until we were at my dad's house."

"I misjudged how close the car was," he said. "I keep Echo on my left to help compensate for the lack of peripheral vision."

"You're incredible, Hudson." Looking at him now, she knew she'd been crazy to ever suspect him of killing Zoey. And if she were honest, she'd admit that her opinion may have been tainted by Corey Robinson. Which made her wonder, just how many of their former classmates were still living nearby? Andrew Barkley had clearly stuck around, but who else?

She scanned the restaurant, looking for familiar faces. Twenty years was a long time, but she'd recognized Hudson and Andrew easily enough.

Her gaze rested on a man wearing a business suit. One of the few dressed so formally in the casual atmosphere. It only took a second to recognize Corey Robinson. Much like Andrew, the years hadn't been kind to Corey. He'd put on weight, his hair was thin, and his complexion was pale. Maybe he was a lawyer or banker—some sort of job that kept him from being out in the sun.

"I see him." Hudson's soft voice had her turning back to face him.

"We should make a list." She took another spoonful of

parfait. Hudson was eating his meal faster than most nurses did. "It won't be comprehensive, but a good place to start."

His jaw tightened, but he didn't say anything. She caught movement from the corner of her eye and glanced over in time to see Corey get up from the table, holding his phone to his ear. He walked outside to take the call. Less than a minute later, Corey returned and caught her gaze. Recognizing her, he smiled and approached their table.

"Kendra, it's good to see you." He gushed as if they'd stayed in touch over the years, when, in fact, Corey had dumped her the moment she'd refused to sleep with him. "You look great."

"Thanks, nice to see you too." She gestured toward Hudson. "You remember Hudson Foster."

"Oh yeah." His congenial tone vanished. "You have some nerve showing up here, Foster."

It was almost exactly what Andrew had said, and she found herself wondering if Andrew had called Corey to clue him in. Beneath the table, Echo began to growl.

Corey stumbled back, staring down at Echo in shock. "You can't have a dog in here!"

"He's a service animal," Kendra said when Hudson remained silent. "I'm surprised to see you're still in the area, Corey. I would have thought you'd have moved on to bigger and better things by now."

Corey puffed up his chest. "I blew out my knee playing football for Colorado State. Went to law school and worked for a big law firm before deciding to open my own office here in town." He pulled out a business card and slid it over to her. "Call me, Kendra. It would be great to catch up again."

She didn't touch the card. "Take care, Corey."

Her former high school boyfriend shot one last angry

look at Hudson before sauntering back to his table. Kendra pushed her empty dish aside. "Let's get out of here."

In answer, Hudson pulled cash from his wallet and set it on the table. She was glad to see he really did have money, but when she reached for her purse, he shook his head. "I've got it covered."

"Thanks." She rose and waited for Hudson to do the same.

"Come, Echo." The dog came out from beneath the table as if grateful to get out of there too.

As they walked back out into the sunshine, she glanced back over her shoulder to where Corey was in deep conversation with the others at his table. "I don't like this," she said in a low voice. "It's wrong the way everyone still blames you for Zoey's death."

"What did you expect?" Hudson cupped her elbow and steered her toward the Jeep. "All the more reason you need to get back into your cute little red car and return to Portland."

"I'm not." She slid into the passenger seat. "You may as well get used to the idea that I'm staying."

Hudson muttered something under his breath as he opened the back for Echo. She didn't care.

It was a shock to realize she was more upset on Hudson's behalf than he was. And if she were being completely honest, she wanted to find the person responsible to clear his name equally as much as she wanted to bring the killer to justice.

HUDSON HAD NEVER BEEN around a more obstinate woman. Kendra was being far too idealistic about all of this.

As if they could really figure out who killed Zoey twenty years after the fact.

He was more concerned with the recent attempts against her, which were likely related to the past. He'd been an idiot to have had breakfast with her at the Corner Café, where the whole world could see them together. He should have stuck to his original plan to keep out of sight.

Too late now.

He started the Jeep and prepared to back out of the spot when Kendra gripped his arm. "Look over there, is that Joe Jamison? He was one of the football players too."

"Yeah." He was a bit surprised so many of the so-called popular guys were still in the area. Twenty years ago, Hudd couldn't wait to get out of Dodge. "Why?"

"Like I said, we need to make a list." She was craning her neck to see Joe, her slender fingers still resting on his arm. *Healing hands*, he thought, and he had to fight the urge to cover them with his own.

"You want me to follow him?" He'd been joking, but she nodded.

"I'd like to know where he works."

He grimaced and shifted the Jeep into gear. Joe headed to a large delivery truck, stepping up behind the wheel. It wasn't a semitruck, but there were soft drink logos stenciled along the side. "He's a truck driver."

"I see that," Kendra said with a frown. She finally removed her hand. "Hudson, is it just me, or do you also find it strange that so many of our classmates are still living here?"

"I do, yes. But then again, most of them didn't have a reason to leave town, the way I did."

"I left too, you know." She sat back in her seat watching

as Joe's truck disappeared around a corner. "Where are you going?"

"You left your car at the shack," he pointed out.

"Please don't stay there tonight. There's a perfectly good motel right there." She gestured out her window. "And there are others if you don't like that one."

It was too early for him to think about where he'd spend the night. For the past few months, he'd taken his life hour by hour, one day at a time, working with Echo to keep him focused. It was only during his extreme migraines coupled with nightmares that he lost track of time. He'd lost twelve hours after one particularly bad episode.

He continued driving back to the old shack where he'd grown up. Kendra had pulled some paper and a pen from her purse and was jotting notes. Easy to imagine her doing the same thing as she worked as a critical care nurse.

Thinking about how she'd lost her daughter and her jerk of a husband put his own injuries in perspective. She'd grown stronger for the adversity, something he needed to focus on as well.

"Did you see anyone else you recognized in the café?" she asked.

He thought for a moment. He'd instinctively taken the seat with his back to the wall, facing the door to watch for threats. But that meant his left eye was facing the main dining room. He'd glanced around, but only to look for signs of anyone carrying a weapon. Then he remembered the young woman sitting near the front with two small kids. "Alyssa Stone and her two kids."

"I didn't notice," Kendra admitted, but she added her name to the list. "Wonder who she's married to."

"No clue." He turned away from the main subdivision and headed toward the dirt road leading to the shack. When he pulled in behind Kendra's red sedan, he threw the gearshift into park and turned in his seat to face her. "Is there anything I can say to convince you to head back to Portland?"

"Nope." She lifted her chin, the same way she had last night. He didn't remember her being this stubborn back in high school. "We should think about where to start looking for clues."

He swallowed a sigh. "We're not detectives working the case."

"So what? No one else is," she shot back. "Besides, you were the one who pointed out that I poked the sleeping bear." She hesitated, then added, "We need to go to the cave."

"No way." He'd already decided to go there, but he didn't want Kendra anywhere near the place.

"I think Zoey had a diary."

He blinked, then stared. "A diary?"

"Yes." She gestured with one hand. "I saw her writing in a small red notebook, but she closed it when she noticed me looking. I asked her about it, and she claimed she was writing poetry."

"Maybe she was."

"No, that's just it. When we were in Ms. Tobin's English class, Zoey kept muttering about how the woman expected us to be future authors the way she kept making us do writing assignments. I think she complained about the short stories too. I should have considered it sooner, but I don't think Zoey was writing poetry. I think she kept a diary."

"Even if she did, it's likely gone now. I'm sure her father and brother would have found it years ago."

"But what if they didn't?" She put her hand on his arm

again. "What if Zoey hid the diary somewhere else? Like maybe in the cave?"

He hated to rain on her excitement. "Think about it, Kendra. The cave is cold and damp. Even if she had hidden a diary in there, it's probably nothing but a pile of mold by now."

"We can't know that for sure," she protested. "And even if it does have some mold, we still may be able to read parts of what she'd written."

"If there's a diary at all."

"Do you have a better idea?" she demanded with annoyance. "If so, I'd love to hear it."

Hudd sighed. "Okay, fine. We'll hike to the cave."

"Thank you." She frowned at him. "Are you always a Debbie Downer?"

The question almost made him smile. His teammates had teased him at times, calling him Hudson the Grouch. "Not always." He shut down the Jeep, reached over and grabbed a flashlight from the arm rest compartment, and handed it to Kendra. He shoved his driver's side door open. "Let's do this."

Kendra jumped down from the passenger seat as he let Echo out of the back. Then he went around to pull his Sig Sauer and MK 3 knife from the glove box where he'd stored them before going into the police station.

"You don't need those," Kendra protested.

He didn't bother to respond. Not only did he have no idea who or what they'd find in the cave, it wasn't that long ago that someone had tried to shoot her. Good thing Idaho was an open carry state. One less reason for Barkley and his officers to haul him in.

Not that Hudd really thought the law would stop the cops from doing whatever they wanted. He took a moment to remove Echo's leash. He didn't want the shepherd to be restricted when entering a potentially dangerous situation.

As they crossed the hilly terrain, Kendra massaged her shoulder. When she noticed his gaze, she quickly stopped. "I'm fine. I did my exercises this morning."

"Good." He knew from Kaleb how important it was to rehab an injured joint properly. As a nurse, he figured she understood that better than most. "I'm sorry if I made it worse."

"You didn't."

The cave was on the other side of the creek. He scanned the ribbon of water, looking for a good place to cross.

Kendra tugged on his arm. "This way. There used to be a few rocks to use as stepping-stones."

"You and Zoey went to the cave often?"

She nodded. "I haven't been there since that night, though."

He felt a little sick at the thought that Kendra could have just as easily been the one who was strangled rather than Zoey. Unless the girl had been targeted for a specific reason? Even so, he had no idea why someone would have wanted Zoey dead.

And he'd thought about nothing but that during the night he'd spent in jail.

The rocks were still there, appearing smaller than they had been. Or maybe it was just his mind playing tricks on him. He crossed the creek first, then waited for Echo to nimbly follow. After his dog reached the other side, he went back to hold out his hand for Kendra.

She took his hand but didn't seem to need his support as she lightly moved from one rock to the next. Seconds later, she stood beside him. "If I'm remembering correctly, the cave isn't far." She gestured with the flashlight toward the larger hill looming ahead.

"Lead on." He gestured for her to go first, mostly so he could cover her six. Not that he could allow himself to notice her sweet curvy backside.

No, sirree. Uh-huh. Off-limits.

Echo lifted his nose to the air, his large ears swiveling from side to side as he picked up on various sounds. He needed to take the dog for a run later; the animal was used to being active. And normally, he ran with Echo to help himself sleep better.

Kendra's steps slowed as they grew closer to the cave. "It doesn't look any different," she said in a whisper.

He hadn't spent much time there, working two jobs had kept him busy. "Maybe you should let me go first—"

The echo of gunfire cut him off. Hudd pushed Kendra toward the cave entrance as the shot had come from behind them. Then he spun and dropped to his knee and fired a warning round before seeking coverage near a tree.

If this guy wanted a fight, then fine. Hudson had never shied away from a threat.

And Navy SEALs always came out on top.

CHAPTER FOUR

Heart thundering in her chest, Kendra landed hard on the cave floor, pain stinging up her arm. She had the fleeting thought as she scrambled deeper into the cave that if this kept up, she'd need more surgery on her injured joint before being able to return to work.

"Hudson!" she called in an urgent whisper. "Are you okay?"

No response.

She drew a deep breath and reminded herself that Hudson had returned fire and was likely hunkered down, watching for more. He was a highly trained Navy SEAL and better at evading bad guys than anyone she'd ever known.

But that didn't mean he couldn't be injured. He'd lost his left eye during his last mission. She'd feel awful if he was hurt again because of her.

Echo trotted over to sniff at her. For some reason, the dog being there was alarming. She'd feel better if the dog stayed close to Hudson.

"Is he okay?" she whispered against Echo's fur.

The dog didn't answer.

Reining in her panic, she crawled toward the opening, feeling along the ground for the flashlight she'd dropped. She found it but didn't turn it on as she huddled close to the side of the cave. In the back of her mind, she knew there could be snakes, bats, mice, or other vermin hiding in the depths, but she tried not to think about it. She focused her attention on listening for sounds of Hudson being out there.

There was nothing but silence.

Easing closer, she risked a quick peek. No sign of Hudson. Her heart thudded painfully, and she swallowed hard. If Hudson wasn't there, it meant he wasn't injured, at least not too badly. The bitter taste of fear coated her tongue.

She knew with every fiber of her being that Hudson had gone after the gunman. Last night he'd done the same, leaving her with Echo. On one hand, it was sweet the way he was so determined to protect her, but she hated the idea of something happening to him.

Please, Lord, keep Hudson safe in Your care!

Kendra watched the surroundings for several minutes, wondering if she dared to use the flashlight or if that would only draw the gunman's attention. She could almost hear Hudson's voice in her head, telling her to stay down and well hidden.

No flashlight.

Echo nudged her with his nose. She rested her hand on his back, grateful she wasn't alone. Her younger self hadn't been frightened of the cave. She and Zoey had come here often, treating it as an adventure.

Being shot at twice and nearly run over by a car was more than enough adventure. All this because she'd mentioned searching for the truth behind Zoey's murder. It hardly seemed possible.

She sat beside Echo for what seemed like forever. Finally, Echo's ears perked forward, and the dog rose to his feet. Seconds later, Hudson appeared in the cave opening. He'd been so silent she hadn't heard him. But Echo had.

"How do you do that?" she asked.

"Practice." He knelt beside her. "Are you okay? Did I hurt your shoulder again?"

"I'll survive." She didn't want to whine about how much it hurt, especially since coming here was her idea. "Did you find him?"

"I found where he stood and caught a glimpse of a black SUV as he drove off." He scowled. "I didn't get his license plate number, though."

"I'm sure black SUVs are fairly common, everyone owns one to drive in the mountains." The thought was depressing. "You're not hurt?"

"No. But I really wanted to find him. He's smart enough and cowardly enough to shoot at us from a distance. It lessens his chance of taking us out but improves his ability to get away without being caught."

A shiver rippled over her. Never in her life had she been the target of someone who wanted to hurt or kill her. It seemed incomprehensible.

"You have the flashlight?"

She was gripping it so tightly her fingers hurt. After turning it on, she passed it over. "I'm hoping Echo will alert us to any animals hiding inside."

"He will. He's a good hunter." Hudson played the beam over the interior of the cave. "So far I'm not seeing any places to hide a diary."

"We'll have to go in farther." She rose. At five feet six

inches tall, she was able to stand, but Hudson was bent over. His shoulders were so wide she wasn't sure how far he'd make it into the cave. She moved forward, a bit surprised that even here the cave looked the same.

"No beer cans or other garbage," Hudson said. "Guess the teenagers don't hang out here the way you used to."

"We didn't have parties in the cave," she protested. "Zoey was the one who never wanted to go home after school. Sometimes we'd hang out here and do homework by flashlight."

He turned to look at her. "Why did she avoid going home?"

"She claimed her brother and father made her do all the work—laundry, cooking, cleaning—after her mother died. She hated being treated like the hired help."

"Hmm." Hudson's gaze was thoughtful. "Makes you wonder if the real killer was much closer to home."

"What?" She gaped at him. That possibility had never entered her mind. "You must be joking. I mean, why would her brother or father kill her? They wanted her to do all the work. Killing her meant they had to do it themselves or hire someone else to do it."

"Maybe one of them found Zoey hiding out in here. They had a huge argument, she was killed, and they worked to cover it up." Hudson played his light along the walls as Echo stayed close to his side. "It would explain why they haven't been able to solve the murder over the years. The only way to truly solve it would have been to frame me for it."

Another shiver rippled down her spine. The scenario he'd described was plausible. "If that's the case, we'll never find the evidence we need. They'll have buried anything that might remotely incriminate them."

Hudson continued to look around. "Maybe, maybe not. No one is immune to making a mistake. And the biggest mistake of all is coming after us now. Frankly, shooting at us and trying to run us off the road only draws more attention to the cold case."

She nodded slowly. "You're right. If the killer would have ignored us, we'd search, likely come up with nothing, then give up and go home."

"Exactly." The corner of his mouth tipped up in a lopsided smile. "Very logical conclusion, Kendra."

His praise shouldn't have made her blush. She hoped the dim interior of the cave hid her juvenile reaction. "On the other hand, the killer may think Zoey left some evidence behind to incriminate him."

"True, but he'd be better off waiting for us to find it before taking us out of the picture, permanently."

"Gee, thanks for that cheerful thought," she said dryly.

Hudson shrugged, then handed her the flashlight. "Where do you think Zoey would have hidden her diary?"

Good question. Looking now, she couldn't even find one possible hiding spot. She forced herself to go deeper into the cave, all the way back to where even she had to crouch to get through. She peered behind rocks and into crevasses, without success.

Frustrated, she pulled on several of the rocks, hoping to pry them up. But they didn't budge.

"Let me try." Hudson joined her, crawling on his hands and knees, with Echo beside him. The dog wagged his tail, nudging his owner as if this was playtime. Hudson managed to move two of the large rocks, but there was no diary hiding beneath.

"I guess I was wrong." She sighed and moved back toward the larger area of the cave opening. Hudson and

Echo quickly followed. "It seemed like the best place for her to use."

"It was worth a try." Hudson stretched his back. "I take it you and Zoey didn't go any farther into the cave?"

"No, we did go back to that space we were just in, but no farther." She swept one last gaze around. "I wonder where her body was found."

"I'd assume in this main area, here. Otherwise, she wouldn't have been found so quickly." Hudson turned to look at her. "Do you remember who found her?"

She frowned, thinking back. "I want to say it was one of the football players. Maybe Joe? When the word went out that Zoey was missing, everyone spread out to find her."

"Hmm." Hudson looked thoughtful. "Maybe we should talk to Joe."

"Well, we know he's a truck driver delivering soft drinks to various stores in the area. Which also means he likely has an alibi for this latest shooting incident." She suddenly wasn't as keen on getting to the bottom of this as she had been. The more she considered the possible identity of the killer, the more she believed Hudson was right when he'd mentioned the football players.

The group of guys had stuck together, something that she had been naive enough to admire. She remembered Corey talking about a party they'd attended the night of Zoey's murder. They'd provided alibis for each other. The worst part of the story was that they'd all been drinking at the party that was held at Coach Donahue's house.

Yet no one had been arrested for underage drinking. Or suspended from the team as a result of breaking the rules.

Instead, the team had won the championship that year.

She was ashamed of herself for dating Corey Robinson and being a part of all that in the first place. Maybe if she'd been more supportive of Zoey, her friend would still be alive.

"Ready to head back?" Hudson's deep voice pierced her troubled thoughts.

"Yeah." She turned off the flashlight. "There's nothing to find here."

Hudson went to the cave opening and scanned the area outside. Then he gestured for her to follow him. Echo sniffed the air, then put his nose to the ground. He went over toward a tree near the side of the cave opening.

"Well, look at that." Hudson followed Echo over and reached up to place his fingers near a hole in the rock. "The bullet is in there."

"Can you get it out?"

He'd already pulled a large wicked-looking knife from his belt and was working the tip against the rock. Moments later, he had a metal fragment resting in the palm of his hand.

Seeing it made her feel sick to her stomach. She was no stranger to the damage a bullet could cause to flesh and bone.

This one had hit far too close.

———

IT WAS PRETTY MANGLED, but Hudd estimated the bullet was from a .38-caliber gun. He placed the fragment in his pocket, then turned to Kendra. "We're going to take the long way back."

Her face was pale as she gave a jerky nod of agreement.

"When we get back to the shack, I want you to head to your dad's place to pack your stuff. There's no reason to stick around, Kendra. It's obvious this guy is going to keep coming after you."

She didn't say anything for a long moment. He noticed she was absently massaging her injured shoulder again. Finally, she said, "He could just as easily find me in Portland."

"Nah, he would have no reason to bother." He was both elated and disappointed that it sounded as if she would be leaving town. Hudd reminded himself that her safety was all that mattered. "He's either a really bad shot or he's purposefully trying to scare us off. If you leave town, and I disappear from view, the killer will relax his guard."

Again, she didn't say anything. He gently guided her to his left as they made their way back to the shack, taking the opposite direction from earlier. Echo pried his way between them as if annoyed that Kendra had intruded on his normal spot.

"I'll pack up my stuff," Kendra said, breaking the silence. "But I'm not going to head back to Portland."

He frowned. "Where are you planning to go?"

"A motel." Her smile was wan. "It's a good idea to make it look as if I'm leaving because that should help keep my dad safe, but I won't leave the area. That way, we can still try to work the case."

A dull ache began to throb in his temple. "Hasn't the past twenty-four hours convinced you that the danger is real?"

"Very much so." Her tone dropped. "It's a sobering realization to know someone wants you dead."

"Then why are you being so stubborn about this?" He couldn't hide his frustration. "What good will it do to stay at a motel? It's not like you can go around town in some sort of disguise pretending to be Ms. Sherlock Holmes."

"I never intended to waltz around in some sort of cheesy disguise." Her tone rose in anger. "Give me some credit, would you? Zoey was my best friend, I want to know what happened to her." She hesitated, then added, "I feel responsible. Like I failed her twenty years ago."

The throb in his temple grew worse. Hudson tried to ignore it, hoping it wouldn't turn into a full-blown migraine. He so didn't have time for that. "The only person at fault is the one who killed her. You sticking around town with a bright red target painted on your back isn't going to help."

"I let Zoey down," she insisted.

"You didn't. Zoey could have come to you with whatever was bothering her, right?" The pain was getting worse, and he could feel his temper start to slip. "Go home, Kendra. If you stay, you'll only get in my way."

"Get in your way?" Her voice rose incredulously. "You're full of yourself, aren't you? Seems to me, I've been helping since the moment we met at the creek. We only came to the cave in the first place because I suggested Zoey's diary might be hidden in there."

His vision began to blur, and he blinked to focus. Arguing with Kendra was only making his headache worse. The woman was more stubborn than any CO he'd ever encountered. And there had been many. Most of them useless.

Except for their senior chief, Mason Gray. Then again, Mason had been in the trenches with them every step of the way. Including their last op.

He tripped over a rock, barely managing to stay on his feet. The pounding in his head intensified. Nausea rolled in his belly, and it took every ounce of willpower he had to keep himself upright.

The shack. He needed to get them back to the shack.

The words echoed in his mind with every thudding beat of pain in his temple. He was so focused on the end goal he could barely manage to watch for threats. He knew there was the possibility of the gunman returning. Especially since they'd left both of their vehicles at the shack.

He stumbled again and felt Kendra wrap her arm around his waist. It bothered him that she had to help hold him upright; he was the one who should be keeping her safe. His role was to protect the innocent.

Like her.

The shack. *Get. To. The. Shack.*

It seemed to be taking forever to arrive at their destination.

Then suddenly they were there. The structure looked blurry, but there was no mistaking the ramshackle place he'd grown up in. The sagging building that didn't hold any good memories, only bad ones. By some miracle, he managed to get inside before dropping to the floor. He couldn't do or say anything else as the pain blocked everything out.

Hudd had no idea how long he remained on the floor, curled in a ball. Time had no meaning. All he could do was internally wrestle with the pain while trying not to moan out loud. Somewhere, deep down, the need to remain silent made him clench his teeth together, holding himself in check.

At some point, he prayed for the pain to stop. If Kaleb had been there, his swim buddy would have prayed for him. Over and over again, he prayed for the pain to go away. He was so far gone that he thought he heard Kaleb's voice reciting a prayer.

But that was impossible as Kaleb was back in Los Angeles with his new fiancée.

Finally, the pain receded to a more tolerable level. His entire body felt as if he'd been run over by a semitruck. Hudd rolled over onto his back, blinking his good eye up at the ceiling. Echo licked his face, and he weakly reached out to stroke the dog.

"Good boy," he croaked. His voice sounded weak, his throat dryer than dirt. He needed to move, to get up and care for Echo, but he didn't want the pain to start up again.

"Easy now." A cold cloth was draped over his forehead. "Don't try to get up yet. Just rest and relax."

It took him a moment to realize the voice was Kendra's. That she hadn't left the shack but had stayed to take care of him.

There was something soft beneath his head. Which was strange because he only had a blanket in the Jeep, one he mainly used for Echo. He blinked again, wondering if he was imagining things.

"What time is it?" He pushed the words through his dry throat.

"Two o'clock in the afternoon. You've been down for a little less than four hours." Kendra slipped her arm beneath his head. "I have a water bottle here. Can you sit up high enough to take a sip?"

Four hours! He couldn't believe he'd been lying there that long. Even more incredible was that Kendra had stayed too. It was the first time he'd had someone beside him during one of these events. Someone other than Echo.

He forced himself up onto his elbows, wincing as the pain started up again. He sipped the water, relaxing as the coolness soothed his raw throat.

He rested back down on the floor, learning more about his surroundings. He was still in the shack, that was no surprise. But he was covered with the blanket and had something soft beneath his head for a pillow. Kendra had gotten Echo's water dish out of the Jeep and had filled it halfway. He hoped the dog had taken some of the water; he'd feel terrible if the animal grew dehydrated.

"Sorry." He rested his good eye for a moment, then turned to look up at her. "The migraines come on without much warning. And even then, the signs are mostly too late to avoid the end result."

"You don't have to apologize." Her features were full of concern. "I was worried about you, Hudson. I can only imagine how much pain you must have been in."

Her sweet caring was a balm to his ragged nerves. He despised feeling weak and helpless, yet somehow, Kendra made him feel as if he was neither of those things.

Even though he clearly was.

"I need a few more minutes." Personal experience had taught him that trying to get up and move too quickly only caused a setback. If the pain came back, he'd never get her safely out of here.

"Take your time." Kendra flashed a wan smile. "If you're hungry, I saved a PowerBar for you. I had a box in my car for the trip between Portland and Boise. I ate one and tried to offer Echo a bite, but he wasn't interested."

"I trained him not to eat people food." He closed his eye again, willing the pain to recede. She was more prepared than any Boy Scout, and he was proud of her for sticking around to watch over him.

Probably for the best that she didn't realize how many nights he writhed on the floor of the shack with no one to help. Well, except for Echo.

"I have ibuprofen too. I know it won't help much, but it can't hurt."

If he had the energy, he'd smile. "Thanks. That's more than I usually take."

"Why is that?" She sounded surprised as she once again slipped her arm beneath his shoulders to help him up.

Once again, he managed to prop himself up onto his elbows. She held out the pills, and he tossed them back. Then she offered another sip from the water bottle. "I just avoid meds in general. You're an amazing nurse."

"Thanks, but there wasn't much I could do to help." She frowned down at him. "How often do these headaches come?"

"Every few days, sometimes less." He knew he needed to get up to make sure there was no danger nearby.

Hopefully a task he could manage without puking his guts out.

He slowly pushed himself into a sitting position. The room spun for a moment, then righted. A good sign. Then he frowned when he realized Kendra had removed her sweater. His gaze shot to her, and he had to smile at the way she had her jacket zipped up to her throat.

"You shouldn't have taken off your sweater for me. I'm used to sleeping on the ground."

"Don't be ridiculous. It was the least I could do." She eyed him warily. "You look a little better, but you're still too pale and shaky. I think you need to eat this PowerBar."

He was about to argue, then realized his hand was trembling. He took the PowerBar she'd unwrapped and took a bite. "Your patients must love you."

She flushed. "Is that sarcasm?"

"No!" He felt awful she'd thought that. "I meant it. You're a great nurse, Kendra. Your patients are lucky to have you."

"Well, some of them love me, until I force them to move

after surgery." A smile tugged at the corner of her mouth. "Then they often swear at me."

"Idiots. You have to move after surgery, or you'll suffer more complications."

"Yes, but I can understand where they're coming from now that I've had shoulder surgery. It's not much fun."

He resisted the urge to touch his damaged eye. It probably wasn't nearly as painful as having shoulder surgery. Or knee surgery like Kaleb had.

The PowerBar settled his stomach. He finished it off, then slowly rose to his feet. "I'm surprised you didn't try to drive to the hospital to get help."

"I planned to, but that was impossible."

He frowned. "Why?"

She sighed. "The wheels of my car and your Jeep were slashed with a knife. We're not driving anywhere."

Slashed by the gunman? While he was lying vulnerable on the floor? He was surprised he and Kendra were still alive. "When?"

"I think it happened while we were in the cave. I found them after you fell to the floor. I couldn't get you up, especially with my injured shoulder." She grimaced. "Looks like we'll have to walk out of here."

Which was probably exactly what the gunman intended. Hudd felt certain the guy might be hiding out somewhere nearby, ready to take another shot at them.

Something he couldn't allow to happen.

CHAPTER FIVE

"Did Echo bark or growl while I was out?" Hudson demanded, moving from one window to the next. "He would know if someone was lurking nearby."

Kendra wished Hudson would sit down as he still looked pale and shaky. Watching him suffer from that awful migraine had been terrible. She'd never felt so helpless. "He growled when we first arrived at the shack. Maybe he picked up the gunman's scent."

"When did you go outside?"

"Shortly after we arrived. I wanted to get the water bottles and the PowerBars." She glanced at Echo who kept pace with his owner. "Echo actually came with me, which was surprising. He sniffed all around the vehicles where the tires were slashed, growling the whole time. But when we came back inside, he stopped growling." The dog's growls had been unnerving, and she'd gotten everything out of the car so that she wouldn't have to go back out again later.

"Good boy," Hudson murmured, reaching down to stroke the dog. "He's a good protector."

"Yes, he is." She'd been amazed at how the dog had

stayed right next to Hudson the entire time he was curled up on the floor. Every so often, Echo would lick his face or rest his chin on Hudson's arm. She'd known the dog had likely done this before, and often. And that Echo wouldn't let anything bad happen to his owner.

The four hours Hudson had been incapacitated had passed with excruciating slowness. She'd considered using her cell phone, but the signal was low, only one bar, and who would she have called? She hated to make her father leave work. And after the recent events at the café, she didn't trust the police.

After seeing the destroyed vehicles, she'd shied away from walking toward the road to get a better signal. The shack was isolated, and she couldn't discount the possibility the shooter was out there. Although she'd been prepared to do that if Hudson didn't get better soon. She'd kept a close eye on his pulse and respiratory rate, which had both been faster than normal.

No doubt because he'd been battling pain.

"Please, sit down for a few minutes. Pushing yourself may cause a relapse."

Hudson glanced at her. "I know, that's happened before. But there's a good chance the shooter is stationed out there somewhere, waiting for us to show ourselves. I need to head out to look for him."

"I'd rather you stayed here, at least for now. Check your phone, I only have one bar. But if you have a better signal, we can call a tow truck."

He stared at her for a moment, then pulled out his phone. "One bar," he said.

Figured. She sighed. "Okay, then we'll need to walk outside a ways, see if we can pick up another bar."

"No, we're not. You're going to stay here with Echo. I'll

head out to find a signal and search for the gunman." The brackets of pain around the corners of his mouth hadn't lessened much. She could tell he was holding himself together with superhuman effort.

"Will you allow me to try something to ease your pain?"

He frowned. "Like what?"

"Pressure points." She wished there was a chair to sit on, but the floor would have to do. "Sit down, I'll show you." When she saw his hesitation, she added, "I don't think it will make your headache worse. And if it lessens some of the pain, it's worth it."

He nodded, then did one more sweep, going from window to window before dropping down to the floor. He was so tall that she had to go up on her knees in order to apply the pressure.

She'd learned the technique through her physical therapist who had also been a massage therapist. Attempting to press on the trigger points on yourself didn't work as well, but she hoped she could ease some of Hudson's discomfort.

"Try to relax," she said in a low voice. Using the pads of her fingers, she pressed hard on the trigger points on his temple, holding the pressure for several seconds before releasing it. Then she moved on to the other trigger points, repeating the applied pressure. She took her time; there was so much tension in his head and neck. Yet as she moved from one spot to the next, she could feel some of that tension easing away.

She finished with the trigger points on the back of his neck. Her knees were stiff and sore, and when she stood, she had to hide a wince.

"That—was amazing." Hudson turned to look up at her, his blue eye full of awe. "I feel a hundred percent better.

Not back to normal, that usually takes several hours, but way better than before you started."

She smiled. "I'm glad. It's a technique some massage therapists use."

"I—thank you." He stood and smiled down at her. It occurred to her that it was the first real smile she'd seen from him. One that lit up his bright blue eye.

"Anytime." Her voice was breathy, awareness shimmering like a living, breathing force between them. Crazy as it sounded, she longed for him to kiss her.

"Kendra." He said her name on a sigh and pulled her into his arms. He didn't kiss her but cradled her close, resting his cheek on her hair. "I'm not sure what to do with you."

She had no answer for that but couldn't deny how much she liked being held by him. His sweetness and caring at odds with his muscular strength. She was secretly glad she'd been able to give him something in return for all the times he'd saved her life.

"I need to go." He released her, taking a step back. It was all she could do not to throw herself back into his arms. "Stay away from the windows. If Echo growls, you need to find a weapon." He glanced around, then handed her the flashlight. "Use this if anyone tries to get close."

"Okay." Hard to imagine hitting anyone over the head with the flashlight, but then again, she'd never been in danger like this before. Feeling grim, she realized she'd likely do whatever was necessary to survive. Even if that meant resorting to violence. Something she abhorred. "Be careful."

The corner of his mouth tipped up in a rueful smile, and she was glad to see the brackets of pain had disappeared thanks to her pressure point relief technique. "Always." He turned to Echo. "Guard."

The dog sat in front of her.

"Good boy." Hudson moved to the back door, the one they'd entered hours ago shortly before he'd collapsed onto the floor. "Remember, stay down."

She lowered herself back to the floor. From this angle, Echo looked huge beside her. Especially his teeth.

Hudson disappeared from her line of sight. Blowing out a heavy sigh, she stroked Echo's fur. As much as she wanted to go along with him, she knew her being there would only be a hindrance. The man moved as if he walked on air, without making the slightest sound.

Kendra told herself to get a grip on her emotions. This teaming up with Hudson was temporary. He didn't live in Idaho, and neither did she. She wasn't sure where he lived and suspected that he didn't have a place to call home. No reason he couldn't make a home for himself in Portland, Oregon.

She rolled her eyes at her foolishness. Even if Hudson was interested, she had no intention of risking her heart ever again. Especially not with a man who could easily have any woman he wanted.

"Temporary arrangement," she muttered to Echo. "That's all this is, right?"

Echo turned his head and licked her face.

"Gee, thanks." She swiped at her cheek. Sitting on the floor might be a way to stay safe, but she didn't like not being able to see what was going on outside. She crawled to the closest window and eased up enough to peer out over the lower sill.

The wind had picked up, the budding tree branches swaying in the wind. She strained to hear other sounds, like that of the gunman, but didn't. And glancing at Echo, watching his ears twitch, she didn't think he heard anything either.

Seeing Echo in action earlier had been impressive. The way he'd crowded her, trying to herd her toward the house while she was grabbing the supplies from her car. It was clear the animal had wanted her inside the shack, where he could keep an eye on her and Hudson at the same time.

If she didn't work twelve-and-a-half-hour-long shifts in the ICU, she'd consider getting a dog. But being left alone that long wouldn't be fair to the animal. Unfortunately, she was allergic to cats.

The minutes dragged by slowly. She found comfort in the dog's demeanor, alert yet calm. She felt certain Echo would let her know if something bad had happened to Hudson.

Yet sitting here doing nothing was driving her insane.

After what seemed like forever, Echo's ears perked forward and his tail began to wag, slowly, then with enthusiasm. She smiled, realizing Hudson would be there any moment.

He came in the front door, and Echo rushed over to greet him, slathering him with doggie kisses. She slowly rose to her feet, resisting the urge to do the same. "Find anything?"

"The spot where the shooter waited." He met her gaze. "No sign of him now, though. At least not between here and the road."

"So now what?"

He looked surprised. "I called a tow truck as you suggested. I had three bars out by the road. He'll be here within thirty minutes with a flatbed trailer. We'll have him take your car first."

"Okay, but I meant what about us? What are we going to do next?"

Hudson eyed her thoughtfully. "It's time for me to get a room at the motel. I like your idea of pretending to leave town, but that won't work until your car is repaired." He frowned. "Something the shooter should have considered before vandalizing the vehicles. Neither one of us can leave until they're repaired."

"Why do you think he did that? I've been trying to understand his angle. The only reason I can come up with is that he wanted us to be stuck out here for a while."

"Yeah, that is strange." Hudson shrugged. "And he had to know that we'd find cell coverage to get help."

"It doesn't make any sense." The lack of logic bothered her; although truthfully, she was grateful the guy hadn't tried to take her and Hudson out while he was writhing in pain. Talk about easy targets.

The tow truck arrived earlier than the promised time frame. He introduced himself as Steve, then scratched his head, looking from her red sedan to Hudson's Jeep. "What in the world happened?"

"Someone has a sick sense of humor." Hudson gestured toward her car. "Let's take care of Kendra's car first."

"You got it." Steve used chains to drag the vehicle up the ramp onto the flatbed. Then he looked at the Jeep. "I'll come back for that one next."

"Thanks." Hudson offered Kendra a hand up into the front seat of the tow truck, then stepped back with Echo at his side. "Steve, will you please do me a favor? I need you to drop Kendra off at her father's house. I'll wait here for you to get back."

"No problem," Steve agreed.

"Are you sure?" She stared at Hudson, feeling a bit lost at the idea of being alone.

"Your dad should be home from work by now if the power company sticks to regular eight-hour shifts. Stay there until you hear from me, okay?"

"Okay." She sat back as Hudson slammed the door. As Steve put the truck in gear and headed down the bumpy dirt driveway, she turned to watch out the back window until Hudson and Echo were no longer in sight.

She told herself there was no reason to be afraid. The likelihood of anyone coming after her when she was in a tow truck was slim to none.

But it was more than that. Deep down, she didn't like leaving Hudson behind. She was becoming far too emotionally attached to him and his faithful companion.

HUDSON DIDN'T LIKE SENDING Kendra off with the tow truck driver, but he felt certain her father would keep her safe long enough for him to get back into town.

"Let's go, Echo." He wanted to take Echo with him to walk the area, hoping the dog might find something he'd missed. His limited vision wasn't his strength these days, and he wanted Echo to have a chance while there was still plenty of daylight.

"I need you to help me out, buddy," he said to the dog. "Alert me if someone is hiding nearby."

Echo eagerly trotted along as he made his way through the wooded area around the shack. Not only was Echo's eyesight better than his, but the dog's nose should help him find what he was looking for.

If there was anything to find.

He tried not to worry too much about Kendra, although it wasn't easy. Three separate attempts to harm her and one act of vandalism indicated someone was truly ticked off about her asking questions about Zoey's death.

If only he could convince her to head back to Portland. Maybe he needed to get her father involved in that conversation.

The thought cheered him up. Not that he wouldn't miss her because he already missed her, and she'd only been gone twenty minutes. He told himself to get over it. Because having her safe was more important than anything else.

Including his ridiculous feelings for her.

He owed her a debt of gratitude for watching over him while he was in the throes of the crippling migraine and again for the way she'd eased the remnants of discomfort with her magic hands.

Healing hands.

As he approached the area where he felt certain the gunman had waited, based on the flattened grass beneath the tree and scuff marks in the dirt, Echo lowered his nose and picked up his pace. Hudd had him off leash to give him room to maneuver.

The dog circled the area, a low growl rumbling deep in his throat. Maybe Hudd was giving the dog too much credit, but he rationalized that it was entirely possible Echo had picked up the same scent near the damaged cars.

"Did you find something?" His tone encouraged Echo to keep going.

Echo stuck his nose beneath some brush, his growling growing louder now. Hudd came over to see what had captured the animal's attention.

At first he didn't see anything, then Echo pawed at the ground. The dog's nails raked up a cigarette butt. The entire end of the cigarette was intact, sloppy in his opinion. Anyone in the military would have fieldstripped it before burying whatever was left deep enough where no one would find it.

Someone on the police force should know that much. Then again, it was entirely possible that whoever had halfway buried the evidence may not have taken Echo's keen nose into account.

Hudson crouched beside the remnant of the cigarette. If this was a true police investigation, he'd ask for it to be tested for fingerprints. At least a partial print would be easily obtained. But based on Andrew Barkley's reaction to him being there, he felt that would be a useless endeavor. No way was the current chief of police going to run this as evidence of a crime. Not without proof.

Hudd had gotten the impression the guy hadn't believed Kendra's story in the first place. Or was trying to cover it up.

Either way was bad news for them.

Hudd lowered himself all the way down onto his stomach to smell it. He was no expert, but the pungent scent of tobacco made him think this had been left recently. Hours rather than days or weeks ago.

The gunman? There was no way to say for sure.

He pulled one of Echo's poop bags from his pocket and picked up the cigarette butt. He'd keep it, along with the mangled slug, even though he knew they wouldn't likely be used to prove anything.

At least, not in Eagle. But at the state crime lab in Boise?

Maybe.

"Good boy," he praised the dog. Echo jumped up, then danced around excitedly. He should have brought one of the dog's chew toys with him but settled for spending a few minutes playing with the shepherd.

When the dog had been suitably rewarded, Hudd set off to continue walking the property with Echo. Finding nothing of interest, he decided to go all the way back to where they'd found the cave. Echo kept his nose to the ground, but unfortunately, the dog didn't growl or act as if there was anything else of interest in the area.

Which made sense, as the gunman had kept his distance when firing at them.

He turned and made his way back toward the shack. As much as he wanted to find the spot where the shooter had hidden, he figured Steve, the tow truck driver, would be returning to pick up his Jeep soon.

He headed toward the road, intending to wait there for the tow truck. It was the best place to get phone service in case Steve got delayed.

And he wanted to check out that spot where the shooter had waited too.

The area remained empty, no sign of anyone hiding nearby. He'd been waiting for less than five minutes when his phone rang. Recognizing Steve's number, he quickly answered. "Foster."

"Hudson? It's Kendra. I—uh, didn't have your number, so Steve let me borrow his phone to call you. I wanted to let you know that I'm fine. I'm at my dad's house, and he just got home from work."

"I'm glad to hear it." He mentally kicked himself for not getting her cell number sooner. Man, he'd been on his own for too long, definitely out of practice when it came to interacting with people.

Especially women. Any normal guy would have gotten Kendra's number right from the beginning.

He cleared his throat. "Do me a favor and call this number from your phone. That way we'll have each other's phone numbers."

"Okay." She disconnected from the call. Thirty seconds later, his phone rang again with a different area code. Probably from Portland, Oregon.

"Kendra?"

"Yes. It's me." She sounded subdued, and he hoped that didn't mean she was upset about something. "Steve wanted me to let you know that he's heading back to pick up your Jeep. We dropped off my car at the local shop first, before he brought me here."

"Okay, thanks." He had no idea why he was grinning like a fool. He'd told Kendra to call him. It wasn't as if this was the beginning of some sort of personal relationship.

Hudd didn't do relationships. He preferred living alone, with only Echo for company. The dog was all the companionship he needed.

"So, you're going to call me when you get into town, right?" Kendra asked. "I wasn't sure what to tell my dad about my car, so I only mentioned a flat tire, not that all four tires had been slashed."

"Yes, I'll call you. We can fill him in on the whole story later. In the meantime, stick close to your dad, and if you see or hear anything suspicious, do not hesitate to call 911."

"I will. And you be careful too. See you later." She ended the call without waiting for a response.

He felt bad she felt it necessary to lie to her father. Should they tell him about the danger? Or go with Kendra's plan of pretending to head back to Portland while going to a motel instead? The latter may be better for her dad in the long run.

The deep rumble of a car engine reached his ears.

Not a sedan like Kendra's but something bigger. Remembering the black SUV that had nearly run them off the road, he moved back from the road, taking coverage in some trees. Ironically, not far from the location the shooter had used.

"Sit," he whispered to Echo.

The dog sat at his side, looking alert. Hudd was glad the car engine appeared to be coming from the right, his good eye catching the glimmer of sunlight bouncing off the silver frame.

Not a black SUV but a gray one. He didn't move, watching and waiting for the driver to get closer. The little he could see through the tree branches obscuring his good eye.

The vehicle rolled slowly down the street. Too slowly, well below the posted speed limit. A warning tingle raised the tiny hairs on the back of his head. It seemed as if the driver was looking for something.

Or someone.

Like him. It wasn't a stretch to believe the shooter had discovered Kendra had returned to her father's house without him. He was beginning to think the shooter had an inside track of information. He couldn't accuse anyone without evidence, but if Andrew Barkley was involved, he could easily have his cops be on the lookout for him and Kendra.

As the vehicle drew closer, he could see it wasn't a police-issued car. But it did have a large spotlight mounted on the dashboard. Not that unusual in the hunting community, many hunters went out to shine deer, flashing them with light at dusk to find where they bedded down for the night.

Seconds later, he dropped closer to the earth, bringing

Echo with him. The driver of the gray vehicle had flashed the spotlight at the area where he was hiding.

There wasn't a doubt in Hudd's mind that the driver was searching for him. To finish the job he'd botched so far.

He barely breathed, waiting with infinite patience for the SUV to move on. Which it finally did.

Still, he didn't move. Echo was stretched out beside him, looking up at him with curious dark eyes. Hudd stroked him reassuringly. The dog didn't mind lying in the dirt any more than he did.

He decided to act as if he were in hostile territory in Afghanistan. He and the rest of their SEAL team had not taken the enemy lightly. The Taliban were very skilled at the art of deception. He stayed where he was, waiting with infinite patience.

A long fifteen minutes later, the gray SUV returned from the opposite direction moving just as slowly as before. He knew the driver, and for all he knew a passenger too, were searching for him. He wished he could see the interior of the car better, but his view was limited.

Yet it wouldn't surprise him to find out the killer had help.

The light played over his hiding spot again. Hudd held his breath, waiting for the vehicle to move on.

It wasn't until he heard the louder engine of the tow truck that he pushed up from the ground and signaled for Echo to join him.

He needed to figure out a new plan and soon. Because whoever had killed Zoey was clearly growing impatient.

It was only a matter of time before he struck again.

CHAPTER SIX

Kendra told her father about the vandalism to her car mentioning only one tire, not all four, as being slashed, while keeping the attempts to kill her and Hudson to herself. Her father was on medication for high blood pressure, and she didn't want to add to his stress. And he would absolutely go off the deep end if he learned about the attempts against her.

Since her mother's passing seven years ago, she and her dad had grown closer. She couldn't bear the idea of anything happening to him.

"Why are you rubbing your shoulder?" he asked with a frown.

She immediately dropped her hand. "Oh, I tripped over a rock and fell on it."

He lifted a brow. "Maybe you should go to the hospital for an X-ray. What if you injured it worse?"

She was very much afraid she had done exactly that. Yet she managed a smile. "I may have to head back to Portland to talk to my surgeon. There isn't anything a doc here can do for me."

"You know best, Kendra," her father conceded.

She didn't like keeping secrets from him. She managed a weary smile. "Thanks, Dad. I hate to leave so soon after coming home."

"Well, you'll still come back to recuperate, right?" He waved a hand. "Best that you get checked out by the experts. And maybe hiking near the creek isn't a smart idea. You can't risk hurting yourself again," he chided. "You were a cheerleader, I'd have thought you could stay on your feet."

"I know, I guess I'm out of practice." Her cheerleading days were long ago, and being dragged to the ground by Hudson to avoid being shot wasn't exactly her fault.

"Are you hungry?" Her dad looked chagrined. "I can order carryout pizza."

"Dad." She tried not to roll her eyes. "How many times have I told you that you should watch your salt intake?"

"Bah, Doc says I'm doing fine." Her dad picked up his cell phone. "I'll grab your favorite, okay?"

She caved, partially because she wasn't the greatest cook on the planet and also because Hudson had asked her to stay here to wait. Ordering carryout pizza was the best way to do that. "Sure, but do me a favor and get two pizzas. I ran into Hudson Foster in town and invited him for dinner."

"Foster?" Her dad frowned. "A bit of a troublemaker, wasn't he?"

"Not really. He worked two jobs all through high school, and the only time he got into arguments was when people treated his mother poorly." She felt guilty for being one of the crowd who'd looked down on him at the time. As if his mother's drinking was his fault. "He's here in town for a short while, so I invited him over."

Her father's frown deepened. "Why would you do that?"

"Because he needs a friend." She was annoyed with his attitude and propped her hands on her hips. "Since when are you so judgmental? Hudson joined the navy after graduation and became a SEAL. He was injured in his last deployment, losing vision in his left eye. I think he deserves respect for the service he provided to our country."

"Well, that's true, and very impressive that he was a SEAL." Her father eyed her curiously. "Quite the coincidence that he showed up here at the same time you've come home to visit."

She couldn't deny it was a huge coincidence. But then again, God was the one in charge, and for all she knew, this was part of God's plan. "Maybe. But I didn't meet up with him in Portland if that's what you're insinuating. We both just happened to come home at the same time."

"Uh-huh." She could tell her dad wasn't convinced. "Okay, I'll order two pizzas. What time is he coming?"

She stared at her silent phone, willing it to ring. "Hopefully soon."

"Should I wait to place the order?" her dad asked. "Wouldn't want to serve your, ah, friend cold pizza."

"No, go ahead." She forced a smile. "It will take at least a half an hour to get the food, and I'm sure he'll be here soon. Oh, and I should mention he has a German shepherd named Echo too."

Her dad held her gaze for a moment before turning away to place the order. As she listened to him, her phone rang. When she saw Hudson's name on the screen, her heart did a weird little staccato beat. She quickly answered it, heading toward her room for privacy.

"Hi, Hudson. Everything okay?"

"Mostly. Echo and I will be heading over to your dad's house soon. Did you tell him anything else?"

She frowned, wondering what he'd meant by being *mostly* okay. "No, I didn't want to worry him."

"Okay."

"I told my dad you'd be here for dinner, he's ordering pizza."

There was a brief pause before Hudson said, "Sounds good, thanks."

"I promise he won't grill you about your intentions," she teased, trying to ease the sudden awkwardness between them.

"I'm not worried. We'll be there soon." He disconnected so quickly she winced. Her attempt at humor had failed miserably.

She took a few minutes to wash up in the bathroom and to change her clothes. It was surreal to realize it wasn't that long ago they were hiding from gunfire in the cave where Zoey's body had been found twenty years ago.

When the doorbell rang, she hurried over to answer it. Hudson stood there beside Echo, who wagged his tail at seeing her. Hudson's expression was far less friendly, his features appearing as if carved in stone. "Steve said he'll have new tires placed on our vehicles first thing tomorrow."

"I'm glad to hear it." She stood back, waving him in. Her dad rose from his favorite rocker recliner chair. "Hudson, this is my dad, Wayne Pickett. Dad, Hudson Foster and his dog, Echo."

"Nice to meet you, sir." Hudson offered his hand.

"Likewise. I hear you served as a Navy SEAL," her father said, shaking his hand.

"Yes, sir." Hudson stood straight and tall without trying to hide his injury even though her father was clearly staring at his left eye prosthesis. "Medically discharged a little over three months ago but served twenty years total, so I've earned my full pension."

"Well, we thank you for your service." Her father gestured toward the sofa where Hudson had slept the night before. "Come in, sit down. The pizza will be here shortly."

She glanced at Echo. "Do you need to feed the dog first?"

Hudson hesitated, then shook his head. "I took care of that before I headed over."

She frowned. Hadn't Steve dropped him off here at the house, the same way he had Kendra? "Will you help me set the table?"

"Uh, sure." He seemed to realize she wanted to talk to him.

Kendra led the way into the kitchen. In a whisper, she asked, "What happened after I left?"

"A silver SUV drove by searching for us." He opened cupboards until he found the plates.

She swallowed a gasp. "How do you know they were searching for us?"

"They swept the area with a large spotlight. Not unlike those used by the police."

A shiver rippled down her spine. Instantly the image of Andrew Barkley's smirk flashed in her mind. "That's not good."

"No." He set the plates on the table, then looked at her. "I really wish you would go back to Portland."

"I really wish you'd stop saying that." She did her best to keep her tone low so her father wouldn't overhear. "We can talk more later about our next steps, okay? And please don't worry my dad with all this. He'd only try to get involved."

Hudson didn't say anything as she pulled out the silverware. When the table was set, they headed back into the living room.

Kendra followed more slowly, her mind reeling with this latest news. She couldn't shake the possibility of Andrew being involved in his sister's murder.

Not that she believed he'd killed her, but maybe he knew more than he'd acknowledged all those years ago.

Which led her back to the football players Andrew hung out with. Including her old boyfriend, Corey Robinson.

She shivered again. The way Corey had sauntered over to talk to her in the café had given her the creeps. She'd wanted nothing to do with the guy, but that alone didn't make him a murderer. Andrew's animosity had been strange too. They'd planned to talk to Joe Jamison, but Hudson's migraine and the tire slashing had put a dent in that plan.

Andrew, Corey, Joe . . . how many others were still around?

They needed to find out, and soon.

She'd been so lost in her thoughts that she hadn't realized her father was giving Hudson the third degree. She inwardly sighed as she sat on the sofa beside him.

"I came to visit my mother's grave," Hudson said. "I was deployed overseas at the time of her death and couldn't make it back."

"They don't give you a leave of absence when you lose a parent?" her father demanded.

Hudson shrugged. "If they can, yes. Depends on what is going on. The missions I was involved with are classified."

"Oh, sure. I understand." Her dad nodded. "What are

your plans now that you're back? Are you looking to get a job?"

"I'm considering my options," Hudson said evasively.

The way her father frowned she could tell he wasn't thrilled with that response.

"You should see how well-trained Echo is," Kendra interjected, trying to change the subject. "Hudson's been working with Echo the past few months, and he's amazing. If I didn't work twelve-and-a-half-hour shifts, I'd consider getting a dog just like him."

"He's a good boy." Hudson reached down to stroke Echo's fur. The dog was stretched out at his feet, but the way his large ears swiveled from side to side, she could tell he was on alert for his next command.

The doorbell rang. Kendra jumped up to answer it. "Pizza's here," she called.

Hudson rose and took the boxes from her hands, carrying them into the kitchen. Echo was his shadow, and her father soon joined them. The spicy tomato sauce and melted cheese smelled amazing, and her stomach rumbled, reminding her they'd only eaten a PowerBar for lunch.

Moments later, they were seated around the table.

"I—I'd like to say grace." She glanced at her father. As far as she knew, he still hadn't attended church since her mother died. "Lord, we ask You to bless this food and the people seated here this evening. We ask for You to continue to watch over us. Amen."

"Amen," Hudson echoed.

Her father hesitated, then softly added, "Amen."

For a moment, tears threatened to spill down her cheeks. Memories of her mother praying before meals were something she'd forgotten about until Olivia had gotten sick. She and her father hadn't talked much about God and faith in those last few days when Olivia had taken a turn for the worse. Her father had arrived shortly after her daughter had breathed her last.

A good three hours before Don had arrived, smelling of heavy perfume with makeup stains on his shirt. It was all she could do not to punch him in the face.

Thankfully, her father had held her close, giving her the support she'd needed.

Maybe there was a way to return the favor. To help her father return to his faith and the support of their church.

But when she caught Hudson's serious gaze, she knew that would have to wait until they'd figured out who was trying to kill them.

HUDD HAD NEVER BEEN good at small talk, even back when he was younger. Kaleb had been the chatty one, while he'd been more content to sit back and watch.

That strategy wasn't working here. Especially since Wayne Pickett was asking him questions as if he were a potential suitor to his daughter. A situation that would be comical if not for the real threat hanging over them. And if not for the way he was inexplicably attracted to her.

Twenty years ago, he would have jumped at the chance to date Kendra. Now, he knew he needed to keep her at an emotional distance if he was going to succeed in keeping her safe. He'd purposefully asked Steve to take him to a motel so that he could make a point of checking in. He'd gone to his room and taken a few minutes to feed his dog, before sneaking out the back with Echo. He'd taken less-traveled side streets to get to Kendra's place.

Hopefully no one would know he was there. After the

way the SUV had searched for him, he'd felt on edge. As if something bad was about to happen.

As if they hadn't had enough bad things going on.

Hudd ate quickly, needing to get Kendra alone for a few moments to discuss their next steps. Since they were both without vehicles, the earlier plan of her pretending to head back to Portland wouldn't work. He figured she'd insist on staying here for the night.

Which wasn't the worst idea, except that he needed to get some sleep. The four hours he'd gotten last night, along with the intense migraine, had already taken their toll. He couldn't protect Kendra or her father if he wasn't functioning at full strength. And he didn't dare leave the two of them alone.

At least he had Echo. The dog was once again sitting at his feet, waiting patiently for them to finish their pizza. He'd been hungry and could tell by the way Kendra was downing her food that she'd been famished too.

"I ran into Corey and Andrew earlier," Kendra said, glancing at her father. "I was surprised they were living here. Do you know if any others from my graduating class are still around?"

"No, but I haven't paid much attention," her father said. "I knew about Corey and Andrew, though, since they've both made big names for themselves."

"Yeah, Corey mentioned he's a lawyer, and I know Andrew followed in his father's footsteps into law enforcement and is now the chief of police." Kendra finished her slice of pizza and pushed her plate away. "I thought I saw Joe Jamison too."

"I don't remember Joe," Wayne said with a frown. "Why all the questions about your old high school friends? Are you thinking of planning a reunion?"

Hudson almost choked on his pizza. The idea of voluntarily reuniting with the classmates who'd mostly treated him like scum was the dead last thing he'd want to do.

"Oh, no, I think our twenty-year reunion was last year," Kendra said quickly. "Don't you remember? They scheduled it for the Fourth of July weekend, and I couldn't get off work to attend. That's a big trauma weekend in Portland, and it was my holiday to work."

Maybe it was wishful thinking on his part, but Hudd got the impression that Kendra had purposefully avoided the reunion, the same way he would have if he'd known about it. Which he hadn't. Not that it mattered as he was in Afghanistan at the time.

Oddly enough, he was glad to know she hadn't wanted to attend.

He stood and carried his plate to the sink. "I'll help with the dishes, then I need to take Echo outside."

"The dishes can go in the dishwasher," Wayne Pickett said firmly. "Go ahead and take care of your dog."

"Thank you." Meeting Kendra's gaze, he jerked his head toward the door. She nodded in understanding.

"Why not take Echo out back?" She dried her hands on the towel. "I'll show you."

Hudd followed her out to the small backyard. Until last night, he'd never been inside her house, but he had gone past the property often enough. The area looked tiny compared to his memories of the place.

Back then, he'd thought Kendra lived in a castle, compared to the shack he'd shared with his mother. Now he realized it was a normal-sized house and that they were hardly rich. It was just that he'd been so poor.

"I'm sorry about my dad," Kendra said quietly. "I don't know why he has the impression there's something more going on between us than friendship. I never gave him any reason to believe that."

"I never thought you did." He tried to smile. "I think it's a rule that a father has to look after his daughter. No matter how old she is."

"Yeah, he means well." She sighed. "I really hate knowing he might be in danger because of me."

"Because of the killer who wants his secret to remain deeply buried," he corrected. "I assume you're staying here tonight?"

"I can't pretend to go back to Portland without a car." She hesitated, then added, "I know I'm asking a lot, but will you and Echo stay too? We have a guest room you can use rather than the sofa. I think my dad will understand your staying here for the night knowing your Jeep was damaged."

He didn't see that he had many options. He could either stay inside or outside the house. After the earlier migraine, he wasn't sure he should push his luck with trying to sleep outside.

"Are you sure your father won't mind?" Hudd glanced at Echo who was watering every tree and bush around the perimeter.

"I'm sure. Besides, I would feel better having you close by. For my dad's sake as well as my own."

"Are you sure you don't want to let him know about the danger?" Hudd made the offer, despite his own misgivings about her dad trying to get involved with the case. He never had a relationship with his dad, who had left shortly after he was born.

"Not yet." She sighed. "Tomorrow morning, after my car tires have been replaced, I'll tell him I'm heading back to Portland to have my shoulder looked at. He knows I fell and injured it. But we'll get rooms at the local motel instead."

"I already have one room booked, I asked Steve to drop me off there. I'm hoping the news gets out that I'm staying there. Which will work against you. Your dad could hear from the town grapevine that you're still in town," Hudd felt compelled to point out.

"I know." She shook her head. "It's a risk I have to take, and something I'll deal with when it happens. I hate lying to him, but I want to be sure he's safe and stays out of this." She met his gaze. "I'm the one who spouted off about why Zoey's murderer had never been brought to justice."

"Stop taking the blame," he said gently. "This is the killer's fault, not yours or mine. Besides, these are exact questions Zoey's father and brother should be asking, not her old childhood friend."

"That part is really bothering me," she confided. "As the chief of police, Andrew should have detectives working his sister's murder in between their other calls. But I don't get the sense he's ever done that."

"No, because it's easier to blame me."

"Okay, but even then, why not continue to search for the truth? Find evidence that points to your guilt?" She shook her head. "It doesn't make any sense."

She had a point. Hudd watched as Echo sniffed the area around the edge of Kendra's yard. "I forgot to mention, Echo found a cigarette butt where the shooter was hiding." He patted his pocket. "I kept it because it could potentially be used as evidence, not that I plan to turn it over to local police."

Her jaw dropped in shock, and she glanced at Echo. "He really found it?"

"Yeah." He couldn't help but smile. "He's a smart dog, pawed at the ground to bring it up from where the perp hid it."

"Too bad we can't prove it's from the killer."

"Tell me about it," he muttered.

"What if we sent it to the state police lab?" Kendra asked. "I'm assuming Idaho has one, Oregon does. We sometimes get trauma cases that come in from highway crashes, which give the state police jurisdiction over the crime."

"A murder here wouldn't be within the state police jurisdiction," he argued. "Although, the FBI has gone in to investigate corruption within police departments."

Her eyes widened. "They have?"

"Yeah." He shrugged. "I don't have any connections there, though." He'd met a couple of federal agents over the years, but none that would remember him. The only thing he had going for him was that his SEAL team had high security clearance. Their last op that had gone completely sideways had been to infiltrate a terrorist cell. A task they'd accomplished.

It was only the extraction that had gotten complicated.

Their teammate Jaydon had paid the ultimate price.

He lightly touched the scar at the corner of his left eye socket. The doc had told him he was lucky the debris didn't get lodged in his brain. He hadn't felt lucky at the time, but he knew that it was true.

His injury could have been so much worse. Being killed was one thing, but living in a prolonged vegetative state would have been so much worse. Yeah, maybe it was time he counted his blessings. Kendra's prayers had helped him realize he had much to be grateful for.

"But we'd need evidence of corruption too," she said, interrupting his thoughts. "Too bad we don't have someone inside the police force that we could trust. I'd love to know what Andrew has done with his sister's cold case file."

"Probably nothing," Hudd drawled. He glanced around, watching as Echo sniffed the perimeter. He'd come to depend on the dog's nose to alert him to trouble.

Thankfully, the dog didn't react the way he did at the bush where they'd found the cigarette butt.

"We should get back inside," Kendra said. "I need to let my dad know our plan of staying here tonight."

He tried to step around her at the same time she turned toward him. The result was that she bumped into him. Hudd instinctively reached out to lightly grasp her shoulders to keep her steady. Then he winced when he realized what he'd done.

"Sorry, I didn't mean to hurt you." He let go of her left shoulder.

"No, it's my fault." She tipped her head back to look up at him.

He had no idea how it happened, but one minute there was a foot of space between them, but the next he cradled her close, capturing her mouth in a deep kiss.

On some level, he'd expected her to jerk away. He wasn't in her league, not by a long shot. But she surprised him by slipping her arms around his waist and holding him tight. She kissed him back in a way that set his entire body on fire.

He couldn't stop himself from deepening their kiss. Never in his life had he wanted a woman more than this.

Kendra tasted like sweetness and sunshine. And it took every ounce of willpower he possessed to break off from her embrace.

Rotten timing. They couldn't do this. Not now.

And maybe not ever. Because as soon as he figured out who was trying to kill her, he'd move on.

Living alone, the way he was meant to.

CHAPTER SEVEN

Kendra was momentarily confused when Hudson stepped back from their embrace. Being held in his arms had made her feel safe and secure. His kiss had wiped all thoughts from her mind, other than his taste, his touch.

She longed for more. Yet the way Hudson was rubbing the back of his neck, looking everywhere but at her, was not encouraging.

Did he regret kissing her? She hadn't imagined the chemistry between them. In fact, his kiss was more intense than anything she'd felt with Don.

"Time to head inside." Was that her voice that sounded so breathless? As if she'd run a marathon instead of kissing Hudson.

Hudson simply nodded and gave Echo a hand gesture that had the dog trotting over to his side.

Once they were back inside the kitchen, she could hear the TV going. Her dad liked to watch sports, despite the fact that Idaho didn't have any major league sports teams. He was a big fan of the Utah Jazz basketball team. She headed into the living room. "Dad?"

"Yeah?" He lifted the remote to mute the sound. "What's up?"

"I offered Hudson the guest room for the night, hope that's okay. His Jeep and my car should be finished at the same time tomorrow, so we can ride together to get them. If that's okay with you."

Her father's gaze bored into hers, as if sensing she wasn't telling the entire truth. "Thought he was staying at the local motel?"

"He is," she hastened to reassure him. She'd been surprised to hear Hudson had checked in at the motel. That he'd gone as far as to ask Steve to drop him off there. "It would just be more convenient if we could share a ride back to the garage in the morning."

He nodded slowly. "Okay, but I expect him to act like a gentleman."

"Yes, sir," Hudson said from behind her. He stepped forward. "You have my word on that."

"Okay." Her father shrugged. "I get up early."

"I told Hudson that. He knows you need to be at work by six." She smiled and bent down to kiss her father's cheek. "Try not to work so hard, okay?"

"Yeah, yeah." He yawned and increased the volume with the remote.

She turned and went down the short hall, pausing to pull two thick towels from the linen closet on her way to the guest room. "Here you go." She set the towels on the edge of the bed. "Let me know if you need anything else."

"We'll be fine, thanks." He stood off to the side, well out of reach.

There was so much more she wanted to say, but she decided to leave it alone. "Good night, Hudson."

"Good night."

She went to her room and blew out a heavy sigh. As much as she'd enjoyed every minute of kissing Hudson, she hated knowing the easy camaraderie between them was gone, replaced with this terrible awkwardness.

After changing into her pajamas, she headed to the bathroom just as Hudson was coming out. They did that weird side-to-side jig before she finally plastered herself up against the wall to give him room to pass.

He paused, then turned to finally meet her gaze. "I'm sorry. I shouldn't have crossed the line with you."

His apology was worse than the awkwardness. "I wasn't complaining, but I understand you're not interested. It's fine. Good night." Without waiting for him to respond, she ducked into the bathroom and closed the door behind her.

After their long day, she didn't mind heading to bed early. She was physically exhausted and emotionally drained. Hudson's kiss replayed over and over in her mind, and she had to shove the memory aside with an effort.

The guy was dealing with enough, no reason to pile on. The terrible migraine must have taken a toll on him, and she told herself to get over herself.

Her feelings were her problem, not his.

She finally fell asleep, waking early the next morning when she heard her dad moving around. Getting a full night of rest felt wonderful, and she quickly climbed out of bed to find her father.

When she walked into the kitchen, she was shocked to see Hudson seated at the table with Echo at his feet. She immediately felt self-conscious about her less-than-flattering flannel pajamas.

"Oh, uh, good morning." She wished she'd stayed in her room. "Everyone is up early this morning."

Hudson nodded but didn't say anything as he sipped

coffee. To give herself something to do, she crossed over to the pot to fill a mug for herself.

"Hudson was telling me about how he lost a teammate in his last operation." Her father frowned. "That must have been very difficult."

She was surprised to hear he'd confided in her father and tried not to feel hurt that he hadn't told her. "I'm sorry to hear that, Hudson."

"Thanks." Hudson didn't meet her gaze.

There was a moment of silence before her dad asked, "You'll call me when you find out what the surgeon says about your shoulder?"

She nodded, hating to lie. "I'm sorry to leave so soon after coming home."

"Well, you'll be back, won't you?" her father asked. "You still can't work for several weeks."

"Yes, I'll be back." She bent to kiss his cheek. "As soon as possible."

Her father patted her hand, then glanced at Hudson. "Are you going with her?"

"No, sir. I'm here for a few more days to get a headstone made for my mom's grave."

"I see." Kendra wanted to roll her eyes at her father's obvious disappointment. "Well, I hope I get a chance to see you again, Hudson."

"Would you like me to make you breakfast?" Kendra asked. "I know I'm not the cook Mom was, but I can make eggs and toast."

"No thanks. I'll stop on my way to work." Her father rose from the table and set his empty coffee cup in the sink. "Take care, Hudson. Kendra, don't forget to call me."

"Will do." She watched as her dad left the kitchen. Then she pushed away from the counter and joined

Hudson at the table. "I hope my dad didn't give you a hard time."

"No, he was fine." Hudson drained his coffee. "I'll make breakfast."

"Really?" She frowned. "Is that because you don't trust my cooking skills?"

"Maybe. But I honestly don't mind." The corner of his mouth kicked up in a half smile, and she was relieved the previous tension between them had evaporated.

"Thanks. I'll get changed." She jumped on the opportunity to take a quick shower and to change her clothes. When she finished, she followed her nose and the tantalizing scents of bacon and eggs to the kitchen.

"Breakfast is ready," he announced. He slid eggs onto a plate, added two slices of bacon, and set it in front of her. "I hope your dad doesn't mind I used some of his bacon."

"I'm surprised he had any in the first place since he eats out each morning." She smiled. "Thanks, this looks amazing."

"No problem." He took the seat across from her, then waited expectantly for her to pray.

"Dear Lord, please bless this food and continue to keep us safe in Your loving care. Amen."

"Amen," he echoed.

The food was amazing, but the domestic scene only made her more keenly aware of their kiss. "We have several hours before our cars will be ready. Any thoughts on what we should do next?"

He nodded. "I need to get Echo back to the motel to feed him, but after that, we should try to track down Joe Jamison. Sounds like he's not as successful as the others. Maybe he's willing to tell us what he thinks about Zoey's murder. And I'd like to know if he was the one who found her."

"I agree." She bit into the crispy bacon. "I remember him as being a decent guy."

"I never did understand what you saw in Corey Robinson."

She swallowed hard. "Looking back, I'm embarrassed that I dated him in the first place. I have no idea what I saw in him back then."

"Maybe it was nothing more than the fact that he was the quarterback of the football team and you were a cheer-leader," Hudson said dryly.

She winced. "Sounds awful when you say it out loud."

"Nah." He took another bite of his eggs. "I understand. Back then, it was all about being part of the popular group."

His comments weren't making her feel any better. "I'm sorry about the way I treated you, Hudson. I really am."

"I haven't thought about high school in a long time." He finished his last slice of bacon. "It's only being back here that brings those old memories back to the surface. And you don't have to apologize. I understand."

"If I could go back and do things differently . . ." She didn't finish the thought. Because, really, looking backward wasn't helpful. Hadn't she figured that out during her divorce? And through Olivia's illness?

"I don't regret joining the navy and becoming a SEAL," Hudson said. He lightly touched the corner of his eye. "Not even after ending up with a fake eyeball."

"You can hardly tell. I'm a nurse, which is the only reason I figured it out so easily." she assured him. She rose and reached for his empty plate. "When I'm finished here, we'll head back to the motel."

"I'll shower, if that's okay with you."

"Of course." She glanced at Echo. "Echo will keep me company, won't you, boy?"

Echo wagged his tail.

Twenty minutes later, they were ready to go. Only Hudson didn't want to head out the front, he steered her toward the back. "Best to keep a low profile," he said.

"Okay." It felt odd to skulk around her childhood home, but she followed Hudson's lead. He took several side streets and even cut through some people's yards to reach the motel.

Using his key card, he accessed the side door of the motel and headed inside. The building had two floors, and the corridors were enclosed with glass. Hudson stopped at the first room at the top of the stairs and quickly gained access to the room.

She followed him inside. The room was clean, yet still smelled a bit musty. Hudson filled Echo's food and water dishes, watching as the dog eagerly dug in to his meal.

"Any idea where to find Joe Jamison?" She asked.

"Yeah, I'm hoping his schedule is such that he'll be dropping off his soft drinks at the same gas station where we saw him yesterday." Hudson glanced at his watch. "Roughly thirty minutes from now."

She was impressed with his reasoning. "Okay, that sounds good."

"I'm going to change, then take Echo out again before we go." He rummaged in his duffel, then disappeared into the bathroom.

Echo finished eating and came over to sniff at her feet. She petted his silky fur, thinking about the upcoming conversation with Joe. She wanted to take the lead since she'd known him better back in high school than Hudson had.

His comment about the cheerleader dating the quarter-back still rankled. Mostly because it was true. At the time, it seemed as if she and Corey were expected to date. And to be crowned homecoming King and Queen.

Pathetic how much that had meant to her back then. For a moment, the image of Olivia's pale, wan face flashed in her mind. She blinked back the sudden tears.

No more crying over her loss. Olivia was home in God's arms. Where she'd stay, pain free, until it was Kendra's time to join her. At one point, she'd prayed that would be soon.

But these past few days had made her realize she wasn't quite ready to die.

"Wait here, okay?" Hudson came out of the bathroom and clipped a leash to Echo's collar. "We'll be back shortly."

"Okay." She sat on the edge of the bed.

Hudson was barely out the door when she heard a voice. "Hudson Foster? I'm Detective Ken Adams, and this is my partner Debra Copeland. We need to ask you a few questions."

"About what?" Hudson asked.

Kendra crept over to the door, which Hudson had left ajar. An uneasy feeling washed over her as she listened.

"We should probably talk about this down at the station," Adams said. "The dog should stay here, though."

"No thanks." Hudson's harsh tone belied the polite words. "Unless you're here to arrest me, you can ask your questions and leave."

There was a moment of silence before Adams asked, "Can you tell me where you were last night around midnight?"

"You came here to the motel to find me, didn't you?" Hudson asked. "Why ask the obvious?"

"Do you know a woman named Jeanie Mayberry?" a female voice asked.

"A woman named Jeanie served me breakfast yesterday at the Corner Café," Hudson replied. "But I haven't seen her since then."

"Can anyone provide an alibi for your whereabouts last night?" Adams asked.

Kendra couldn't stand it. She swung open the door, surprising the trio. "I can. Hudson and Echo stayed overnight at my father's house last night."

The detectives looked dumbfounded by her presence there. They looked at each other, then back to her. "And you are?"

"Kendra Pickett. My father is Wayne Pickett, he works at the power company. He can verify Hudson was with us last night too. What's this about Jeanie Mayberry? I was with Hudson when she served us at the café."

"She was murdered. Her body was found in the cave across the creek." There was a hint of annoyance in Adam's tone. "I'm going to need you both to come down to the station to provide statements."

"We just gave you our statements," Hudson said. "And again, I have no intention of coming down to the station."

The detectives looked as if they weren't sure what to do next. Finally, Adams pointed his finger at Hudson. "Stay in town," he ordered. "Or I will get an arrest warrant to take you in. Understand?"

"I don't plan to leave town," Hudson said calmly.

"Me either," Kendra piped up.

"Good." The two detectives turned and left. She watched, feeling sick to her stomach. Jeanie's murder changed things. She didn't like the way Hudson was being set up for her murder. They had to do something and soon. Before he was thrown in jail, possibly for the rest of his life.

———

HUDD HAD FIGURED things couldn't get much worse.

He'd been wrong.

Yet on some level, he wasn't surprised. In fact, his efforts to make sure he was seen checking into the motel last night paid off.

The detectives obviously knew he'd been staying there. So did the real killer.

The same man who'd struck again, killing their young server in cold blood, hoping Hudd would be a suspect as he'd be alone in the motel room.

The killer had no idea he'd stayed with Kendra instead.

"Come inside," Kendra said, tugging on his arm. "We need to call a lawyer."

"Not Corey Robinson," he said as he followed her inside. "And why did you speak up about being my alibi? You made it sound like we spent the night together."

"I know, but I was afraid they'd haul you off in handcuffs." She planted her hands on her hips. "This is serious, Hudson. You need a good lawyer, not Corey but someone else. The real killer is setting you up to take the fall."

"I'm aware." He sighed and rubbed the back of his neck. He felt certain that his arrest wasn't imminent, thanks to Kendra claiming to be his alibi. Granted, she hadn't lied; he had stayed at her house for the night. But he could have easily slipped out to kill Jeanie, returning before she knew he was gone. Something he wasn't about to tell either of the detectives unless he absolutely had to. "Let's go. We still have time to chat with Jamison."

"Wait a minute." She tightened her grip on his arm. "Let's find you a good lawyer first. I'm worried they'll come back to arrest you."

"Not with you as my alibi," he countered. "Besides, I think it's clear we've made the killer nervous. Why else would he strike again, putting the body in the same place where Zoey was found? Even a blind man could figure out that he's trying to set me up to take the fall. Something the detectives should consider."

"Unless Andrew is feeding them a line of baloney," she muttered darkly.

"True." He lightly covered her hand with his. "Try not to worry. If I need help, my SEAL teammates will come at a moment's notice."

"Why not call them now?" She was really digging in her heels over this. "I'm worried about you."

Her concern was sweet but unnecessary. "They're not going to arrest me with you as my alibi. We need to talk to Jamison. The best way to clear my name is to find the real killer. Trust me on this, okay?"

"Okay, okay." She finally nodded and released his arm, although her expression remained troubled. "Let's go."

He paused at the door, then turned to face her. "I don't expect you to lie for me, Kendra. If I am arrested at some point, I don't want you to lie about spending the night with me."

She flushed, and it was all he could do not to kiss her again. "I won't. But how insane is it that someone actually believes you'd kill a random café server."

"Not entirely random," he countered. "She was young and had long dark hair like Zoey. I'm sure the real killer chose her because of that."

"Both Corey and Andrew saw us at the café with her," she said slowly.

"Along with dozens of other citizens," he felt compelled to point out. "Come on. Let's get out of here. We don't want to miss Joe."

She nodded and followed him and Echo outside. This time there were no detectives to stop him from heading back down the stairs and out the rear door of the motel.

He glanced down at Echo who trotted happily alongside him. The dog hadn't reacted in a negative way toward the two detectives. Remembering how the dog had growled at the location where the shooter had stood made him wonder if Echo might be able to sniff out the killer.

Something to consider, although he doubted he'd be able to convince a cop that Echo could ID the guy by his scent.

He thought briefly of Bravo, Mason's K-9 partner. Bravo had been their scent dog over in Afghanistan. The K-9 had helped them find several tangos, even the leader of the Taliban house they'd infiltrated.

Should he give Mason a call? He knew the senior chief wouldn't hesitate to come join him. However, he didn't have anything for Bravo to use as a scent source. And there was a part of him that didn't want his former leader to know he'd once been considered a suspect in Zoey's murder.

He decided against making the call as he led the way to the gas station located catty-corner from the café.

It bothered him that Jeanie had been murdered. He felt certain that she'd been used to throw suspicion off the real killer and onto him. A pawn in a sick, deadly game.

"Hudson? I think that's Joe's truck." Kendra's voice broke into his thoughts.

"I see it." He was glad his hunch had paid off.

"Let me talk to him," Kendra said. "I'm less threatening than you."

That made him want to grin. "You can be fierce, Kendra. But I agree he's more likely respond to you in a positive way."

"Here goes," she said as they grew closer. Hudd held back a bit, turning away and giving Echo the signal to stay, as she hurried forward. "Joe? Hey, it's me, Kendra Pickett. I was in your chemistry class with Mr. Johnson, remember?"

Joe glanced over his shoulder, eyeing Kendra with interest. "Oh yeah, hi. What brings you back to town? Heard you were a nurse in Portland."

Hudd crouched beside Echo, trying to make it look as if he wasn't listening intently to the conversation. He found it interesting that Joe knew where Kendra had ended up. He doubted any of his former classmates knew he was a Navy SEAL.

Not that it mattered. He couldn't care less what they thought.

Not entirely true, he silently admitted. He didn't like being accused of murder.

"I am, but I injured my shoulder, so I came home to stay with my dad for a few weeks." Kendra smiled brightly at Joe. "I didn't realize you were still in the area."

Joe shrugged. "Don't want to leave since my kid is still here."

"Oh, are you married?" Kendra asked.

"Divorced from Denise." He grimaced. "My son is worth it, though. Joe Junior is a great kid."

"I'm sure he is," Kendra gushed. "I remember Denise, she was one of the cheerleaders on our squad."

"Yeah." A wistful expression crossed Joe's features. "Those were the good old days."

"I ran into Corey and Andrew, but are there other class-mates of ours that are still in the area?" Kendra asked. "I couldn't make the reunion last year because of my job. I was hoping I could meet up with a few while I'm home."

Hudd had positioned himself so that Joe and Kendra were visible from his good eye. He noticed a hint of disgust cross Joe's features when she'd mentioned Corey and Andrew. A sentiment he agreed with.

"I don't see those guys much," Joe said. "Dave Nevins is still around, I think he's a cop, too, like Andrew. The only one I've kept in touch with is Mitch Cooper. He's married now, to Alyssa Stone."

"Oh yes, Mitch was in our chemistry class too. He didn't play football, though, did he?"

"No." Joe's tone was curt. "There were times I wished I hadn't made the team."

That captured Hudd's attention. Joe sounded as if he'd had a falling out with Corey Robinson and Andrew Barkley. Maybe even with Dave Nevins too. He only had a vague memory of Joe. The guy had been pretty quiet, unlike Corey and Andrew.

"Why would you say that?" Kendra asked in surprise. "I thought you were all friends."

"Not really." Joe shrugged.

"Is it because you found Zoey's body in the cave?"

Joe blanched. "That was Dave, not me." He moved to step past her. "Look, it was nice chatting, but I have to go. I have a schedule to keep."

"Wait, can I ask one more question?" Kendra put a hand on his arm. "Please? It's important."

"I guess." Joe looked at her warily.

"Look, I know this is going to sound crazy, but do you

think it's possible that Andrew, Corey, or Dave had anything to do with Zoey's murder?"

Joe's reaction was visceral. He gaped, stumbled backward with a look of panic on his face. "I don't know anything! I have to go." He jutted around Kendra, jumped up into the driver's seat of the truck, and slammed the door behind him.

Well, Hudd thought. *Isn't that interesting?* Guilt had practically oozed from the guy's pores.

Joe knew far more about what his former football player teammates had done back then than he was letting on.

CHAPTER EIGHT

"That was weird." Kendra stared at the back of Joe's truck as Hudson and Echo came over to stand beside her. "He acted as if I'd slapped him."

"He knows something," Hudson murmured.

"I'm not sure he *knows* anything," she argued. "Otherwise, why would he keep silent all this time? He doesn't hang out with the old crew anymore; there's no reason for him to keep their secrets."

"They could have threatened him or his son. Or maybe he suspects one of them killed Zoey but doesn't have any proof." Hudson put his arm around her waist. "Good to know Nevins was the one who found Zoey's body. Let's go. We're supposed to stay out of sight."

"Yeah." She allowed him to steer her back toward the motel. The idea of hanging out in his room, though, held little appeal. Talking to Joe convinced her that one of the football players very well could be involved in Zoey's murder. "I should have taken Corey's card. I need to talk to him."

"No way, that's a bad idea." Hudson's arm tightened

around her. "He's a slick lawyer, accustomed to using his words to twist the truth to his advantage. Do you really think he'll slip up and say something incriminating?"

He had a point, but that didn't mean they shouldn't try. "If I get him to talk about old times, he might give me some insight into what may have happened that night." She hesitated, then added, "I could play up how the police came to question you about Jeanie's murder. Pretend I believe you might be involved."

"Not happening." Hudson's flat tone irked her. "Stay away from him."

"Who died and put you in charge?" she shot back. "The whole reason I'm staying in town is to find out the truth. Jeanie's murder makes that more imperative than ever. I hate that she died for no good reason other than to frame you."

"We don't know that's the reason." From the corner of her eye, she could see the muscle tick at the corner of Hudson's jaw. He was angry but was doing his best to hold his feelings in check. She admired that about him, but that didn't mean she was going to blindly follow his lead.

She couldn't help feeling as if they were living on borrowed time. That the detectives would return at any moment to put Hudson in cuffs and haul him to jail. They needed to do everything possible to prove his innocence. Including setting up a meeting with Corey Robinson.

One thing she'd learned about arrogant surgeons is that they believed they were more skilled and smarter than everyone else. Which sometimes resulted in them blowing off a nurse's concern about a patient. She'd gone over a surgeon's head more than once and had been proven right on all but one occasion. She hadn't cared about the blowback, some surgeons couldn't handle being wrong, but her patients were her top priority.

Somehow, she felt certain arrogant lawyers would be the same way. Corey would likely act cool and confident. But maybe she could still find a way to rattle him, maybe put a dent in his overblown ego.

It was too early in the day, though, to approach him. Hadn't he said something about getting together for a drink? She'd find him online to set that up.

Unfortunately, she couldn't come up with a way to corner Andrew Barkley. Unless . . . she abruptly stopped and pulled out her phone.

"What are you doing?" Hudson asked.

"Looking to see if Andrew is married." She scrolled through social media until she found Andrew's page. He had a wife, Sasha, and two kids. When she switched to Sasha's page, she didn't see any employer listed. Some people didn't bother to include that kind of information, but she could easily imagine Andrew encouraging his wife to be a stay-at-home mom.

"So what if he is?" Hudson urged her forward toward the motel. "I highly doubt his wife is going to know anything about what happened twenty years ago."

"Sasha was one of our classmates, two years behind us." She tucked her phone away and followed Hudson into the motel. "It can't hurt to talk to her."

Hudson sighed heavily as Echo bounded up the stairs to the second-floor motel room. "You can't just go talking to people willy-nilly. We need a plan."

"Yes, we do." She had the start of one already forming in her mind.

Hudson unlocked the door, then stepped to the side to

let her in. Echo brushed against her legs on his way to slurp from his water dish.

"I'd like to try to talk to Joe again," Hudson said.

She took a seat on the edge of the bed. "Why do you think he'll talk to you?"

"I don't know for sure, but he knows or suspects something, so it's worth a try. I'm the one under suspicion, maybe I can use guilt to force him into cooperating."

"Maybe, although he didn't seem to be willing to talk just now." She figured it couldn't hurt to try. "We should also talk to Dave Nevins."

"He's a cop and likely loyal to Barkley," Hudson said. "For all we know, he's the one who has been shooting at us."

"Any of these guys could be the one shooting at us," she argued with annoyance. "Except for Joe Jamison, I think he's more afraid of the actual killer."

Hudson didn't say anything for a long moment. She could tell he didn't like the idea of her being a part of this. "I'm going to see if Corey will have a drink with me later. I'd like you to stay somewhere close while we meet."

"I don't want you to meet with him." Hudson's steely blue eye locked on hers.

"I understand, but you shouldn't underestimate me. I work with surgeons every day, I think I can hold my own."

Hudson dropped his chin to his chest. Echo came over to rest his head on his owner's knee as if sensing his distress.

"Please, help me do this," she said softly. "I'll feel more comfortable if you're someplace close watching over me."

After what seemed like an hour, he finally raised his head, glum resignation in his gaze. "Fine. Where exactly do you plan to meet him?"

It was a good question. She wasn't familiar enough with the town to know which pubs and taverns had survived over the years. "Do you think Flannigan's Irish Pub is still around?"

"No clue." Hudson gestured to her phone. "Look it up."

She did and was surprised to see Flannigan's was indeed still open for business. Then she remembered it was one of the places where Hudson had worked while they were in high school. "I'm sorry, I forgot you used to work there. I can try to find somewhere else to meet."

"Why? It's fine." He waved a hand. "I didn't mind that job. It was only when my mother would show up and start drinking that things turned ugly."

She winced. Taunts and slurs had often been aimed at Hudson and his mother. "I hate knowing how poorly you were treated back then."

He shrugged. "No point in living in the past. I've endured far worse during several deployments overseas."

Humbling to realize how Hudson's troubled youth had helped mold him into the impressive man he was today. He was right. There was no point living in the past.

Olivia's smiling face flashed in her mind. Yeah, some days were easier than others.

"I think I can find a place inside the bar to hang out while you meet with Robinson," he went on. "The interior is shaped like a sideways L. The main bar takes up most of the space, but there's a small alcove off to the right where I can watch without being seen."

She nodded. "Okay, that works. I'll give him a call later."

"I was thinking about Dave Nevins," Hudson went on. "It would be interesting to know his work schedule. The silver SUV was a personal vehicle, not an unmarked cop ride. I don't have any social media accounts, but can you look him up on your phone?"

"Yes." She entered Dave Nevins name, but nothing came up. Then she went back to Andrew's account and found him as a friend under his full name, David Nevins. She held up her phone. "Want to see a recent photo?"

Hudson nodded and sat beside her on the bed. His musky male scent reminded her of their heated kiss. "Is that him?"

"Uh, yeah." She cleared her throat and forced herself to concentrate. "He's aged better than Corey, that's for sure."

"Yeah," Hudson agreed absently. "I wonder if he did some time in the military."

She quickly scrolled through several photos, finding one of David wearing army green. "You're right, he did."

"I thought so." Hudson met her gaze. "Could be that Dave has more integrity than Andrew or Corey."

"Just because he was in the army?" she asked doubtfully. "I'm pretty sure bad guys end up in the service."

"They do, but his record must be clean if he was able to get a job as a cop." He blew out a frustrated breath. "I could call my senior chief, see if he can find out more about Nevins's background in the service."

"Would they really talk about their former soldiers?" she asked.

"Doubtful." The corner of his mouth tipped up in a wry smile. "Who would have thought I'd miss the ability to get inside intel?"

"I'm sure it hasn't been easy for you to adjust to civilian life," she murmured. "Twenty years is a long time to serve."

"Is there anything in his social media that indicates when he was discharged from the army?" Hudson asked. "I'm assuming he didn't have a medical discharge since he made it through the police academy."

She scrolled through the information, which thankfully

wasn't restricted by privacy settings. Something she found a little odd for a cop. Many of the cops she'd met while working in the trauma ICU made a point of staying off social media.

Given the unrest over the past few years, she couldn't blame them.

Boise wasn't Portland, and the smaller towns functioned more like social networks anyway, so it was possible that David wasn't too worried.

"Here, looks like he got out about ten years ago." She showed Hudson a photograph of David being sworn in as a newly minted cop. "Maybe you're right about him. He's still a suspect because he found Zoey's body, which may have been because he'd known where to look. It can't hurt to talk to him."

"That's what we thought about Joe," Hudson said wryly.

"True." She glanced at the time. "How much longer before we pick up our vehicles? I'll feel better about my dad's safety when I can pretend to leave my father's house to head back to Portland."

"Should be soon." Hudson stared at her. "There's still time for you to change your mind about returning to Portland."

She rolled her eyes. "I won't." They sat in silence for a few minutes until her phone rang. Recognizing Steve's name on the screen, she quickly answered. "Hi, Steve."

"Hey, your sedan and Hudson's Jeep are ready to be picked up."

"Thank you. We'll be there very soon." She disconnected from the call and stood. "Let's go."

"Do you mind walking?" Hudson asked as he strode toward the door. "It's only a mile from here."

"Not at all." She jumped to her feet, glad to have an excuse to move. Bedside nursing was hard work with long hours of standing on your feet. But having surgery made her realize that sitting around with nothing to do was far worse.

The route Hudson chose kept them off the main thoroughfare. When they arrived at the garage, Hudson spoke to the service man first, then came out to hand her the keys to her car. "It's all set."

She frowned. "Where do we pay?"

"I took care of it."

"Why would you do that?"

"Because I wanted to thank you for supporting me during that migraine."

"I don't need to be repaid for helping you, Hudson. I'm a nurse. I could never leave someone lying in pain."

"I'm still grateful." He gestured toward her car. "Head back to your father's house and pack your things. I'll wait for you at the motel. Make sure you drive around back, that bright red car is fairly noticeable."

"I will." She slid behind the wheel, hoping and praying this plan would work. Her dad was the only family she had left in the world. She couldn't bear the thought of him being in danger.

HUDSON OPENED the back of his Jeep for Echo. The dog nimbly jumped inside. As he walked around to the driver's side, he frowned when he noticed Joe's truck rumbling past.

Without hesitation, he jumped inside the Jeep and followed him.

He didn't own a fancy phone, but he was able to shoot

off a quick text warning Kendra he might be late meeting her at the motel. When she texted back asking why, he simply said they'd talk later.

Tailing Joe's truck wasn't difficult, it was large and easily seen from a distance. Of course, that worked against Hudd too. But he doubted Joe knew he drove a blue Jeep. He didn't believe the guy was the one who'd shot at them, tried to run them off the road, or slashed their tires.

But he felt certain the guy knew something that would help them get to the bottom of Zoey's murder. And these recent attempts against them.

He expected Joe to be headed to his next drop-off location, but the guy pulled up in front of a small white house. Using the binoculars, he watched as the guy hurried inside.

Moments later, Joe emerged with a kid who looked about ten or eleven years old. He also had a small suitcase in one hand. Fear was etched on Joe's features, and Hudson knew his hunch about the child being in danger was dead-on.

No wonder Joe had reacted so strongly to Kendra's question about Zoey's murder.

All roads lead back to Andrew Barkley and Corey Robinson, he thought grimly. Who else would have the power to instill that level of fear? So much so that Joe was getting his son out of harm's way.

It bothered him that the kid was in danger. He'd spent his entire adult life protecting the innocent. He shoved open his car door and ran over to where Joe was helping his son get inside.

"I'm a former Navy SEAL, and I can protect your son."

Joe's eyes widened. "Hudson? How did you find me?"

"The truck." He stepped closer. "I know you're scared,

and I don't blame you. But I can protect you and Joe Junior if you help me."

Indecision flashed across Joe's features. "I'm just taking Joey to see his grandparents in Boise."

"The only problem with that plan is Andrew, Corey, and the others know who your parents are. It wouldn't be difficult for either of them to use their respective resources to track down your family."

Joe's shoulders slumped as he realized Hudd was right.

"I don't understand what's going on, Dad," Joe Junior said. "Why this sudden rush to get me to Grandma and Grandpa's house? I'm only off school today and tomorrow. I have to be back on Monday."

"I can help protect you," Hudd repeated. "I have a German shepherd named Echo who is a great guard dog."

After what seemed like an eternity, Joe reluctantly nodded. "Okay, but we have to hurry. I don't want to take any chances."

"Agree." Hudson gestured toward the truck. "Leave this here for now. I'll drive both of you to a local motel. We'll have you stay there until it's safe."

"Are you really a Navy SEAL?" Joey asked.

"Yes." Hudd met the boy's gaze. "I know you must have questions, but we can talk later. After you're safe."

"Why are you doing this?" Joe asked as he and the boy climbed into the back seat of Hudson's Jeep.

"Because kids shouldn't be used as pawns," Hudd said curtly.

"You're right. They shouldn't." Joe stared down at his hands for a long moment. "Thank you."

Hudd met his gaze in the rearview mirror. Echo sniffed at Joe and his son through the crate. He was glad the dog didn't growl. "Neither should women. Did you know that

Kendra Pickett has been shot at twice and nearly run off the road?"

Jamison paled. "Why?"

"Because she's been asking questions about Zoey's murder. Like why it hasn't been solved over the past twenty years." Hudd drove to a different motel from the one he was staying in. Going back to the same place where the detectives knew his room number wasn't smart. "We need to understand what happened back then. Before there's another attempt to hurt Kendra."

Jamison looked at his son, who was momentarily preoccupied with Echo. "Nice doggy," Joey murmured.

"I don't know anything about Zoey's death," Joe protested.

Hudd didn't believe him. "You know enough to get your son out of harm's way."

Jamison winced. "My son is the most important person in the world to me."

Hudd nodded. "I can understand that. But are you willing to stand by and watch more innocent women die?"

Jamison turned to stare out the window. When Hudd pulled into the parking lot, he shifted the Jeep into park and killed the engine. "Stay here. I'll get a room for you."

"Okay," Jamison agreed.

Hudd went inside, secured two connecting rooms, then hurried back outside. He drove around the back of the motel, parking near the dumpster. "Let's go. We'll get Joey settled with a movie, then we'll talk."

Jamison didn't argue. Hudd texted Kendra to let her know the change in plans. She sent back a thumbs-up emoji.

"Is there a swimming pool?" Joey asked.

"Afraid not." Hudd handed Jamison a key. "Unlock the connecting door when you get in."

After entering his own room, he unlocked the connecting door. Finding the other side still locked, he lightly rapped on it. Echo sat beside him. After a few minutes, Jamison pulled the door open. "I found a Star Wars movie for Joey to watch."

"Good." Hudd stepped back and gestured for Jamison to join him. "Echo, come."

The dog wagged his tail and followed Hudd into Jamison's room. Joey was stretched out on the bed, his eyes glued to the TV. "Guard, Echo."

"He can stay with me?" Joey asked in surprise.

"For now, yeah." He left the boy and dog together, returning to his room. A few minutes later, his phone rang. "Yeah?"

"It's me," Kendra said. "Which room are you in?"

"One ten." He disconnected from the line. "Kendra will be joining us."

Jamison blew out a breath, looking nervous. "I don't really know anything," he said again.

Hudd held up a hand to stop him. "Enough. You either cooperate with us, or I'll drop you and Joey back at your place. You can take your chances with your parents watching over him."

"I thought you said kids shouldn't be used as pawns?" Jamison protested.

"They shouldn't. But this is serious, Jamison. Jeanie Mayberry has been murdered, and I have no intention of letting Kendra become the next victim."

A knock at the door interrupted whatever Jamison was about to say. Hudd peered through the peephole, then opened the door for Kendra.

"I don't understand," Kendra said, glancing between them. "What's going on? Why is Joe here?"

"His son is in the next room," Hudd informed her. "Echo is watching over him." Then he turned to Jamison. "Why don't you explain why you felt the sudden need to get Joey out of town?"

Kendra gaped in surprise. "You did?"

"He was planning to take him to his parents in Boise, but I convinced him to come here instead so that Echo could help keep them both safe."

Jamison stood and began to pace. "I overheard some of the guys talking after Zoey's murder. They didn't know I'd come into the locker room that following Monday, and they were laughing over the fact that Hudson was the prime suspect in Zoey's murder."

"Old news," Hudd said curtly. "Go on."

"One of the guys mentioned you had an alibi," Jamison continued. "But Andrew said that wasn't true and that Hudd would be arrested for Zoey's murder."

The guy wasn't telling him anything he didn't already know. Hudson reined in his temper with an effort. "Then what?"

"One of them asked what would happen if you weren't arrested." Jamison's voice had dropped to a whisper. "Someone else said that no matter what happened, they needed to stick together."

"They, meaning the football team?" Kendra asked.

Jamison nodded. "The star players of the football team," he clarified. "Then Robinson said that the truth didn't matter."

Hudd could barely control his frustration. "That hardly seems enough to make you haul Joey out of town."

Jamison collapsed onto the edge of the bed. "Robinson

said the truth didn't matter because it would never come to light. Whether you were arrested or not. That's when I dropped one of my shoes, the cleats made a loud sound on the floor. Andrew came over and found me standing there. He dragged me to the others, demanding to know what I'd heard."

"What did you tell them?" Kendra asked.

"I tried to bluff my way out, but neither Corey nor Andrew believed me. Andrew grabbed me by the shirt and slammed me against the wall. He pushed so hard I had bruises all over my chest the next day, worse than when I played in a game." Jamison swallowed hard. "He told me that I needed to keep my mouth shut about whatever I over-heard because snitches ended up dead."

Hudd glanced at Kendra, hoping she'd reconsider her plan to meet with Corey later. "So why do you think your son is in danger?"

"Because Robinson chimed in. I don't remember his exact words, but it was something along the lines of if you don't care about yourself, think about what we'll do to your family." Jamison lifted his hands. "They were mean back then, and that hasn't changed over time. I'm not about to take any chances. Not with my son."

"I don't blame you," Kendra soothed. "I would feel the same way."

Hudd scrubbed his hands over his jaw. The fear in Jamison's eyes was real, but his information wasn't much help.

The only thing they could say for sure was that one of the football players had to be responsible for Zoey's death.

But which one?

CHAPTER NINE

One of her classmates had killed Zoey. And Jeanie too. Nausea rolled in her stomach at the possibility of Corey being the murderer. She'd dated him. Kissed him. Made out with him.

Thankfully she hadn't slept with him. Which was the reason he'd dumped her.

Not that she'd been heartbroken. Quite the opposite. At the time, she'd felt an overwhelming sense of relief. She was headed to college in Portland on a partial scholarship anyway, so she hadn't missed him at all.

She met Hudson's gaze and could read the concern reflected there. He'd want her to forget about her idea to get information from Corey, but she couldn't do that. If anything, it was more critical than ever to talk to him.

"You're sure you don't have any idea who murdered Zoey?" Hudson pressed Joe. "Why would her own brother want to cover up his sister's murder?"

Joe stared down at the floor for several moments. "I don't know why Andrew would want to cover it up unless he was the one responsible. But I swear I have no idea which one of them killed her."

"Who was there that day you overheard them talking?" Kendra asked. "Andrew and Corey, but who else?"

"Tristan, the coach's son, and Ben," Joe admitted.

She frowned. "Not Dave Nevins?"

Joe shook his head. "No, he wasn't there. To be honest, he was one of the nicer guys in the group."

"Tristan Donahue and Ben Clemmons," Hudson said thoughtfully. "Do you know if either of them are still in town?"

"Tristan is, but I haven't seen Ben Clemmons since graduation."

Kendra used her phone to look up Tristan. She remembered him as being very stocky but fast, the way a good running back should be. Coach Donahue had always bragged about how Tristan, Andrew, and Corey were the stars of the team. Andrew had been Corey's favorite wide receiver, and Tristan had been the bulldozer, plowing his way through the defense. "Found him," she said. "He's bald now."

Joe ran his hand over his thinning hair. "We can't all look as good as you two."

"I wasn't trying to be mean, just that I may not have recognized him if I passed him on the street." She tried to backpedal. "Looks like he works at the local bank." She remembered the guys who were seated at the table in the café. "Do you think he's still chummy with Andrew and Corey?"

Joe nodded. "I've seen them hanging out sometimes."

"Anyone else we should consider?" Hudson asked.

"No. They were the ones who hung out together the most. I don't think they'd have included the other guys in anything illegal. Other than minor stuff like underage drinking or smoking pot," Joe added.

Three suspects. "Thanks for telling us," she said softly. "We need to get to the truth in order to stay safe."

"But Hudson is going to protect Joey, right?" Joe asked, glancing between them.

"We will, yes." Hudson nodded toward the connecting door. "Why don't you go watch the movie with your son? Kendra and I need to talk for a few minutes."

He hesitated, then rose and moved toward the door. At the threshold between the two rooms, he glanced back at Hudson. "I'm sorry I wasn't nicer to you back then."

Hudson waved a hand. "Don't worry about it."

Joe ducked inside the connecting room. Hudson went over to close the door partway before turning to face her. "Robinson and Barkley are at the very top of my list of suspects."

"Agree, although it seems crazy to think Andrew killed his own sister. But don't even think of asking me to hold off meeting with Corey. We need to do something proactive, and I know you'll keep me safe."

His jaw tightened, and the muscle tick was back. "He's dangerous."

"I know." She wasn't going to downplay the threat. "But we'll be in a public place. Besides, he hasn't even agreed to meet yet."

"You called him?"

"I left a message," she confirmed.

He grimaced and looked away. She could tell he was hoping Corey was either too busy or uninterested enough to get back to her. "I need to return to my old room to pick up my stuff and Echo's food and water dishes. I'd like you to stay here until I get back."

"That's fine." She absently rubbed her injured shoulder. "I'll do my exercises while you're gone."

Hudson left without saying anything more. She went through her physical therapy recommended routine, wincing at the tightness of the injured joint. She silently prayed the damage wasn't bad enough to require more surgery.

Her thoughts whirled around what Joe had told them. He'd actually heard four football players talk about sticking together to hide the truth. There had been no evidence that Zoey had been sexually assaulted, so she didn't think they'd all ganged up on her.

But something happened, and the killer used his closest friends to cover his butt.

She agreed with Hudson. Corey and Andrew seemed the two most likely suspects.

As if on cue, her phone rang. Her heart shot into triple digits when she recognized Corey's number. She drew in a deep breath, let it out, and lifted the phone to her ear. "Hello?"

"Kendra, it's Corey. I was glad to hear you called." His smooth tone put her teeth on edge. "I'd love to take you out for dinner tonight."

Dinner? She cast her mind around for a good excuse. "Oh, I'm sorry, but I have plans with my dad. I'd love to meet you for a drink, though, say around seven? It's been a long time since I've been back to Flannigan's Irish Pub."

"I can do better than Flannigan's," Corey said. "Louisa's Lounge is a very trendy place in Boise."

"Oh, I don't want to go that far." She never imagined Corey would be this difficult. "I really had my heart set on Flannigan's."

There was a pause, and she could imagine him

frowning at not getting his way. "Sure, that's fine. We can meet at Flannigan's at seven." His voice dropped. "I can't wait to see you again."

It was all she could do not to gag. "I'm looking forward to catching up. See you tonight, Corey."

"Later, babe."

Babe? She punched the end call button on the phone with more force than was necessary. Corey clearly suffered from an overblown ego, and she was already dreading their so-called date. Their interaction made her wonder if it would be worth it. As Hudson had pointed out, Corey wasn't likely to share anything incriminating with her.

Yet she had to try. As she continued doing her exercises, she considered how to approach the man. Catering to his ego would be a good way to start, along with bringing up some of their happier memories from the past.

She remembered that Zoey had been murdered one week after homecoming. She'd been working at the grocery store as usual, until closing time, then she'd watched a movie with her dad. She and Corey hadn't been together because Coach Donahue had thrown a party for the players.

Something that had provided a good alibi for each of them, unlike Hudson who only had his drunk mother to vouch for him being home.

Was there a way to trick Corey into revealing more about that night? She wasn't sure how, but she hoped something would come to her.

After she finished her exercises, the motel door opened, and Hudson came in carrying two duffel bags. Echo came running from the connecting room, overjoyed to see him.

"You're supposed to be guarding Joey," Hudson admonished the dog. He set down his things, rubbed the animal's pelt, then went back to the connecting room. "Guard," she heard him say sternly. "Guard Joey."

She smiled, imagining Echo reluctantly stretching out on the floor near the boy. She knew the shepherd would protect them from anyone who threatened them.

When Hudson began unpacking Echo's things, she said, "I'm meeting Corey at seven at Flannigan's. He tried to get me out for dinner, then he wanted to go to some fancy place in Boise, but I held firm."

He grunted, his displeasure reflected on his features.

"I remember it was a Saturday night when Zoey was killed, she was found on Sunday morning. It was a week after homecoming, the guys were all at the coach's party. I'm going to see if Corey will tell me more about the night at Coach Donahue's house."

Hudson shrugged. "Good luck with that."

"Oh, I think he'll try to brag a bit, which may help." She refused to let him drag down her spirits. "Come on, Hudson. You have to admit it's worth a try."

He didn't say anything for a long moment. Then he rose to his feet and crossed over to her. "The only thing that matters to me is that you're safe."

She reached out to take his hand. "I feel the same way about you. I still think those detectives will be back with an arrest warrant for Jeanie's murder."

"I saw them outside our previous motel," he admitted. His warm hand gently cradled hers. "They obviously want to be sure I don't leave town."

The news made her stomach clench with worry. "I don't like it, Hudson. Andrew is the type to act first, then ask questions later."

"Just like his old man," Hudson agreed. "Keeping me in jail all night just because he could."

She scowled. "That's terrible."

"Yeah." He surprised her by drawing her hand up to his mouth for a kiss. "We're going to work on some nonverbal signals for you to use tonight in case things go south."

"Ah, okay." The sweet kiss had distracted her. "Although I doubt he'll try anything hinky in a public place."

"Don't bet on it," Hudson replied darkly. He released her hand, then gestured to the sofa. "If you need me to show up and drag you out of there, put your hand up to your neck like this." He demonstrated what he meant.

"Got it." She hoped she didn't make the gesture by accident. "Anything else?"

"Keep your phone handy. If I see something off, I'll text you."

"I don't know about that. I'd rather you didn't interrupt unless it's critical. Especially if he's on the verge of confiding something about that night."

"I need you to trust me," Hudson said firmly. "I won't interrupt unless it's important. But I don't trust this guy, and I need you to pay attention to what's going on around you." He paused, then added, "Add me in your phone as Dad."

"I already have dad in my phone," she protested.

"Add his first name to his number instead," Hudson insisted. "This way, my text won't appear threatening to Robinson if he happens to see it."

"Fine." She pulled out her phone and did as he asked. "Anything else?"

"Just pray nothing goes wrong."

"It won't." She put as much assurance in her voice as possible, despite the curl of dread at spending more time with Corey unfolding in her stomach.

She'd pray for safety as much as she'd pray for information to help them find the actual killer.

Before he struck again.

HUDSON STILL WASN'T happy about Kendra's plan, but at least she'd gone along with his safety measures. He didn't trust Robinson one inch.

"I'm hungry," Joey said from the connecting room.

Hudd moved over to meet with father and son. "I'll pick up something for lunch. What would you like?"

"Fried chicken!" Joey cried.

"No, we had that for dinner last night," Jamison admonished. "How about burgers from your favorite fast-food restaurant?"

"Okay," Joey agreed. "Can we go there to eat?"

"Afraid not, we need to stay here," Jamison said.

"Where is the danger coming from?" Joey wanted to know.

"Nowhere in particular. You and your dad are safe here," Hudd said. "There may not be any real danger, but we're just being extra cautious, okay?"

"I guess." Joey looked frustrated. "But I'd rather be playing with my friends."

"I know, and you'll get to do that very soon," Jamison assured him. "Just hang in there for a while, okay?"

"Yeah, yeah," Joey grumbled.

Hudd could tell the novelty of watching movies was already wearing thin. He took their food order, then went to get Kendra's too.

"Maybe I should go," she said. "You need to stay hidden from the detectives for as long as possible."

"No need, they won't find me." He wasn't that worried about the pair. "I'll be back before you know it."

She sighed. "Fine, but if you're not back in thirty minutes, I'm going to head to the police station to find you."

The image of her stalking into the police station to rescue him almost made him smile. "I'll call you if I'm delayed for some reason."

He left the motel, easing along the corner to sneak out through the back of the building. The setup here wasn't as nice as the previous motel, but the situation couldn't be helped. He knew it was only a matter of time before he was arrested. Once that warrant was issued, the detectives would realize he'd checked out of the motel. They'd send a BOLO out for him, which would make it that much more difficult to stay under the radar.

If he were alone, it would be easy. He'd been here for a week without anyone knowing. But that was before the added responsibility of watching over a kid, the kid's father, and Kendra.

He managed to get to the fast-food restaurant easily enough, but he had to wait fifteen minutes for the order to be fulfilled. As he was about to leave, a police cruiser pulled into the parking lot.

Hudson turned and left the restaurant from the opposite door. Outside, he hesitated, then risked a glance at the cop who entered.

Unfortunately, it was a cop he didn't recognize. He'd hoped to run into David Nevins, the former army veteran. Too bad, he had no idea if the guy was even working today.

He kept his head down while taking as many shortcuts as possible to get back to the motel. They gathered in Jamison's room to eat, and he hid a smile when Joe Senior looked surprised when Kendra insisted on saying a brief prayer before they ate.

"Dear Lord, we ask You to keep us all safe in Your care," she said.

"Amen," Hudd echoed.

"Amen," Jamison finally said. His son simply shrugged and ate a few french fries.

"Is Echo a purebred German shepherd?" Jamison asked as they ate.

"Not a purebred, no. But you can tell by looking at him he's predominately shepherd," Hudd replied.

"He's smart and would make a great police dog," Kendra added loyally. "Hudson has been training him for months."

"I can tell. I've never been around a dog this well behaved," Jamison agreed.

Hudd didn't like leaving Echo behind, he'd gotten used to having the dog as a companion. Yet he also knew Echo's skills were needed to protect Joe and his son while he was out working the case.

And keeping an eye on Kendra later that evening.

The rest of the day passed slowly. He asked Kendra to pull up Nevins's social media page again, but there was no way to know where the guy lived. Or what his work schedule was. Frustrating, but he certainly understood. There was no way he'd ever put himself out on social media.

Mostly because of the classified missions he'd partici-pated in. And the possibility of Taliban leaders tracking him down.

From that perspective, it surprised him that Nevins had an account.

When he couldn't stand sitting around a moment longer, he stood and turned toward Kendra. "I'm going to check Flannigan's. Make sure there haven't been many changes since I worked there."

"I'm sure there have been," she said with a frown. "I know it was relatively new back then, but the owners likely made updates over the years."

"I just want to check it out," he repeated. "All successful missions start with detailed planning. Stay here. I'll be back soon."

"Fine." She blew out a breath. "But don't be too long. I just realized I should probably wear something nice tonight. Corey made it sound as if this was a date."

The pang of jealousy was stupid and unwelcome. "You look fine," he said gruffly. "And you wouldn't wear a dress or anything fancy to an Irish pub."

She opened her mouth to argue, but he slipped out the door and quietly closed it, effectively ending the conversation.

Despite admiring Kendra more than any woman he'd ever met, he also found her to be the most exasperating female on the planet. He figured some of that came from her career choice. He could easily imagine her standing protectively in front of her patient while arguing with a surgeon.

And maybe it was juvenile, but he did not want her to dress up for this meeting with Robinson.

The pub was on the other side of town, so it took him nearly twenty minutes to get there. He went around to the back door, the way he used to go in and out when he worked there.

The first person he saw was Ralph Rizzo, the cook. Ralph had seemed old back when he'd been in high school, but the guy looked even more ancient now. He was shocked to find Ralph still working, although he was grateful to see a friendly face.

"Hey, Ralph, how are you?"

"Huh?" Ralph squinted at him through thick glasses. "Foster?"

"Yeah, it's me," Hudd said, pleased the cook remembered him.

"What are you doin' here?" Ralph asked with a wide smile. "Figured you'd move on to bigger and better things by now."

Ralph had been one of the few residents who'd actually spoken positively about Hudd's future. He was the father figure Hudd had never had, and looking back, he knew he was fortunate to have worked alongside him. "I joined the navy and became a SEAL."

"No way!" Ralph's grin widened. "I knew you would do good once you got outta here."

"Yeah." Hudd glanced around. "Is the place still owned by Hugh and Mary?"

"Yep. Although their son Bobby has taken over managing the place." Ralph grimaced. "He's okay, I guess."

Hudd hoped that wouldn't be a problem. "I can't stay, but I wanted to stop in to say hi." He gestured toward the door leading into the restaurant. "Mind if I take a look?"

"Go ahead." Ralph turned back to his work. "I'd ask you to stay, but I'm getting ready for the dinner rush."

Hudd gave the old man a one-armed hug, then made his way through the kitchen. It hadn't changed much, and when he opened the door an inch, he noticed the restaurant looked much the same too.

Okay, that was helpful. He moved back through the kitchen, noticing several curious gazes on him from young employees who didn't know him. Which was fine. He preferred anonymity these days.

Outside, he noticed another police cruiser rolling past. The hairs on the back of his neck lifted in warning. During the week he'd been here, he hadn't noticed many police cars. Now he'd seen two in a matter of hours.

Hudd decided to take a detour to his previous motel. When he arrived there, he frowned when he noticed the detectives were gone.

Not good. He had a bad feeling things were moving faster than he'd anticipated. Based on the increased police presence, it seemed likely that an arrest warrant had been issued, and every single cop in the city was looking for him.

This would make it extra difficult for him to hang out at Flannigan's while Kendra met with Corey Robinson.

Yet he wasn't going to let this stop him from watching over her. He may need to adjust his plan a bit, but he'd be there.

No matter what.

Hudd used all the skills he'd learned through his SEAL training to take yet another detour, this time to purchase new clothes. He needed something other than his typical jeans and T-shirt attire, as well as some props.

Pleased with his purchases, including Joey's fried chicken for dinner, he made his way back to the motel he'd stashed Jamison and his son. The first thing he noticed was that Kendra had changed into a hot pink sweater, which enhanced her pretty features.

"What's in the bags?" she asked. "Besides food."

"New clothes and some baby powder to make my hair look gray." He shrugged. "Just taking a few extra precautions."

She nodded. "I trust you, Hudson."

The statement made him feel warm and gooey inside. He did his best to ignore it. The next two hours passed slowly. When it was within forty-five minutes of the time she was scheduled to meet with Robinson, he ducked into the bathroom to change.

When he emerged, Kendra gasped. "How did you do that?"

He couldn't help but grin. "It's amazing what baggy clothes, a slouch, and gray hair and a ball cap can do to change your appearance. I'm hoping no one who sees me will look twice." It was a trick he'd learned in Afghanistan. He'd been forced to dress like the Taliban on more than one occasion.

And he knew from personal experience that people tended to avoid looking at those who appeared down-trodden.

He'd been ignored for years, thanks to his mother's drinking problem.

"I'm going to get settled inside about twenty minutes before your scheduled meeting," he told Kendra. "Please be safe, okay?"

"I will." She impulsively hugged him. "Thanks for being there for me."

He held her close for a moment, thinking he'd do just about anything for her. Then he released her and headed back outside.

He entered the pub, managed to find a seat at a small two-top table that had a good view of the bar, then settled down to wait.

Silently praying with all his heart that God would keep Kendra safe tonight while she faced off with the snake known as Corey Robinson.

CHAPTER TEN

Corey entered the pub right on time, appearing out of place wearing his fancy suit. Kendra inwardly cringed while pasting a fake smile on her face as he approached. She had no idea why she'd ever found him attractive, but then again, she didn't look the same as she had twenty years ago either.

"Kendra," he gushed, leaning in to kiss her. She tipped her head so that his lips brushed her cheek. "You look amazing."

"Thanks, you look like you just came from court. Long day?" she asked, feigning interest.

"Yes, I had court earlier this morning." he sat on the stool, his knees brushing hers. It took all her willpower not to grimace. "I represent some very high-profile clients."

No surprise he'd started out bragging already. "Sounds interesting."

"I can't talk much about their cases, but I will say my line of work is never boring." He gestured to get the bartenders attention. "What would you like?"

"A glass of chardonnay, please." She didn't drink much, but she did enjoy white wine on occasion.

"I'll have a glass of Macallan Scotch on the rocks, and the lady would like a chardonnay."

"We don't carry Macallan, sir. Only Johnnie Walker." The bartender was clearly irritated with Corey's request, as if this wasn't the first time Corey had asked for a particularly expensive Scotch.

Corey's lip curled, but he nodded. "I guess I'll have the Johnnie Walker, then." He tossed a fifty-dollar bill onto the bar, and Kendra could tell all of this was his pathetic attempt to impress her with his money. Little did he know she'd walked away from Don when he was making half a million a year, asking for nothing from him other than the house she'd paid for during the years he'd been a resident.

What did money matter when your daughter was dying of cancer?

The bartender filled their order, but she didn't immediately reach for her glass. "So you're a defense lawyer then?"

"Yes. I started in the DA's office, but the pay was ridiculously low, so I didn't stay long. I'm glad I switched, being on the defense side of the aisle is much more lucrative and interesting."

She would have had more respect for him if he'd have stayed in the DA's office, but she wasn't about to mention that. The goal for this evening was to convince Corey to talk about himself. Starting with now, then hopefully going back in time to when they were younger.

"I'm sure it is," she agreed. "It's funny, I don't remember you being interested in going to law school back when we were about to graduate high school."

He shrugged. "We were kids then. I wasn't sure what I wanted to do with my life. It was only after I got serious about college that I decided to study law."

She wanted to ask if that was specifically because he'd

broken the law by taking someone's life or covering up the truth about a crime, but again, she held her tongue. She couldn't be too blunt, or this evening would end in a matter of minutes. Besides, his comment opened a path for her to probe the past. She reached out to lightly touch his arm. "I'm sure Zoey's murder played a role in your decision. Such a terrible tragedy."

"It did, yes." He was a better actor than she would have given him credit for. His expression was full of compassion. "Zoey deserved better than what Foster did to her."

"I guess it's a good thing you and the other football players were all together that night," she said. "At least, I think you were all together. Isn't that what you told me?"

"Of course we were together," Corey snapped. His expression changed as if he realized he sounded defensive. "I'm really glad that Coach Donahue threw that party for us at his place," he continued. "Otherwise some of us may have been suspects in her murder too."

"That's right, you were there with the others," she said thoughtfully. "I think you mentioned Andrew Barkley, Joe Jamison, and Tristan Donahue."

"That's right." Corey eyed her over the rim of his glass as if trying to understand why she was talking about this. "The entire team was invited because of how well we were playing. Even then, he knew we'd end up going to state."

It had been exciting at the time, but she didn't point out that they'd lost the state championship because Corey had thrown an interception in the end zone. She hid a smile as she kept the conversation on the night of Zoey's murder. "But I don't think they all made it to the party, did they? I seem to remember seeing David Nevins at the grocery store while I was working." It wasn't true, and she fully expected to be called out on her lie, but that didn't happen.

"Oh yeah, Nevins couldn't make it," Corey said with an exaggerated frown. "I forgot."

Her pulse spiked, and she clenched her hands in her lap as she realized what he'd done. There were only two reasons he would have gone along with her lie. Either he knew a few of the guys weren't at the party that night and figured one of them was Nevins or he'd been somewhere else himself.

Her instincts were leaning toward the latter.

"I wish I could have been with Zoey that night." She glanced up at Corey from beneath her lashes. "If I had been there, she might be alive today."

"You don't know that," Corey protested. "Foster could have found another day to kill her. Everyone knew the guy had a bad temper."

She desperately wanted to support Hudson's claim that he hadn't touched Zoey, but of course, that would defeat the purpose of this meeting. "Maybe, although he was never charged with her murder."

"No." Corey's tone was curt. "He should have been. It's hard to believe Chief Barkley failed to make a case against him. If I'd been the prosecutor, I'd have thrown the book at Foster. He'd be serving a life sentence right now."

By faking evidence? She hoped her thoughts weren't reflected on her features. "I'm sure you would have."

She caught a glimpse of Hudson across the room, sitting in an alcove type of area. It made her remember she hadn't pulled out her cell phone. She turned and rummaged in her purse to find it. Of course, the stupid thing had dropped all the way down to the bottom of her bag, so it took a few minutes for her to retrieve it.

When she looked up and set her phone on the top of the bar, she realized Corey had her wine glass in his hand. "You haven't touched your drink," he said, offering it to her. "Try it, if you don't like it, we'll find something better. I'm sure this place isn't known for having fine wines."

She took the glass but still didn't take a sip. For some reason, his persistence irked her. When she saw him looking at her phone sitting on the bar, she added, "I'm expecting a call from my dad."

"Aren't you a little old for him to be checking in on you?" Corey asked with a leering smile. "Besides, your old man always liked me, I'm sure he's happy to know we're reconnecting."

She couldn't believe how full of himself Corey was. "Oh, Dad has been very supportive since my divorce. Although I didn't realize you were divorced, Corey. Aren't you still married to Lynette?"

"We're separated," he responded quickly. Too quickly. She didn't believe him for a hot second.

Her phone buzzed, and she glanced over to see Dad a.k.a. Hudson had sent a text. She quickly scooped up the phone before Corey could read the message.

Robinson drugged your wine.

She blinked, read the text again, then lifted her gaze to Corey. She held on to her temper with an effort. Had he really slipped her a roofie? What kind of scumbag was he anyway? She wanted nothing more than to bust him, but instead, she lashed out with her hand, knocking the wine glass over on the bar. The glass shattered, and the contents spilled everywhere. Corey jumped off his stool, backing away from the bar so as not to ruin his oh so expensive suit.

"Oops. So sorry. I'm such a klutz."

"I—uh, it's okay." Corey managed to pull himself together. "I'll order you another one."

"No thanks, I'm really sorry, but I need to go. My dad isn't feeling well." She frowned and shook her head. "I'm worried he has heart issues. I'm hoping to get him a referral to one of our cardiologists in Portland." She stood and slipped her phone back into her purse. "Sorry to cut this short, Corey. Maybe we'll have a chance to see each other again sometime?"

"Anytime, babe," he said, leaning toward her as if intending to kiss her.

She offered her cheek, then quickly moved away before he could try anything else. Skirting around several tables, she headed outside, not stopping until she reached her car. Only then did she realize how badly her hands were trembling.

He'd tried to drug her. It was so unbelievable, yet she didn't doubt Hudson's claim. It had been odd the way he'd been holding on to her wine glass after she spent a few minutes searching for her phone.

She opened her car door and climbed inside. Gripping the steering wheel with both hands, she took several deep breaths attempting to pull herself together.

Maybe she should have accused Corey of drugging her drink. Made a big stink, demanding the contents be tested.

This couldn't be the first time Corey had pulled such a stunt. How many other women had he drugged, then raped? Because that was the reason a guy drugged a drink in the first place, right? To get a woman into the sack?

She couldn't stop shaking. Swallowing hard, she started the car and forced herself to drive back to the motel.

The worst part of all was that she hadn't gotten any definitive information from Corey. All she'd done was prove Hudson right.

If Hudson hadn't been sitting nearby close enough to watch over her, she knew the night would have ended very differently.

Kendra abruptly pulled off the side of the road, opened her car door, and lost the entire contents of her stomach in one sickening lurch.

HUDD HAD BEEN COMPLETELY SHOCKED when he'd noticed Robinson putting something in Kendra's wine. Not that he was surprised the guy would do something so despicable, but drugging her wine here in a crowded pub had been a huge risk.

Yet, the bartender hadn't noticed. Corey had chosen the right moment, when Kendra was rummaging in her purse and the bartender was busy serving others.

When she'd purposefully knocked her glass over, Hudd had wanted to jump to his feet and cheer. But, of course, he'd stayed where he was, waiting for Kendra to make her next move.

Thankfully, she'd ended their evening, moving quickly away from Robinson. He didn't blame her one bit. The guy was lower than a snake in the grass, a slug on the bottom of the river.

Hudd had intended to follow Kendra back to the motel, but when he realized Robinson wasn't leaving, he'd changed his mind and remained seated.

So far, no one inside the pub seemed to have recognized Hudd. Wearing the baggy clothes, adding the powder to whiten his hair, and pulling the rim of his cap low over his brow had proven to be good camouflage.

He continued to watch Robinson. The guy had turned to survey the occupants of the restaurant bar area as if scouting for his next victim.

Robinson was a sexual predator, no question about that.

But was he also a murderer? The two didn't necessarily go hand in hand. Even so, the guy should be in jail.

It was difficult not to go shake him down to find the vial of whatever date-rape drug he had tucked in that pricey suit coat. Hudd decided to wait and watch, see if he tried the same thing with someone else.

Fifteen minutes later, Robinson pushed away from the bar and headed toward the door. Hudd followed him. He easily identified the car Robinson drove because it was a flashy sports car, so he ducked around the corner of the pub to get into his Jeep. By the time he pulled around, he could see the flash of Robinson's taillights as he pulled out of the parking lot.

Keeping a couple of cars between them, he followed Robinson all the way to a house located a few miles from Kendra's father's place. It didn't take long for Hudd to realize Robinson had gone to see his old buddy Andrew Barkley. There was a large silver RAM truck in the driveway. Barkley's personal ride? Or someone else's?

Interesting that he'd come here. Had Kendra rattled the guy with her questions about the past? Did Barkley know Robinson drugged women to force them to sleep with him?

He parked down the block from the Barkley house, trying to decide if he should wait here to see where Robinson went next or head back to the motel to meet with Kendra. He knew she had to be upset about what Robinson had tried to do. And he was curious as to what she may have found out during their brief conversation.

He was about to put his Jeep into gear and leave when the door of Barkley's house opened and Robinson came back out. He looked angry as he stalked back to his sports car and slid inside. Moments later, the guy drove off, tires squealing as he hit the gas.

No way was Hudd going to let him find another victim. He needed to know where the guy was headed. He pulled away from the curb and followed.

This time, Robinson headed toward downtown Boise. Feeling grim, he watched as Robinson pulled into the parking lot of Louisa's Lounge. Moments later, the guy disappeared inside.

His current attire of baggy clothes, baseball cap, and gray hair would stick out like a sore thumb in a place like this. Yet he couldn't bear to stand by and do nothing while some poor woman fell victim to Robinson's vile assault. He needed a plan.

A woman wearing what appeared to be a uniform paused outside the door to Louisa's Lounge to light a cigarette. Peering through the window, he could see the bartender inside was wearing a similar outfit, white shirt, red vest, black pants.

Perfect. He pushed open the door of the Jeep and hurried over. "Excuse me, do you work in Louisa's?"

"Yeah, why?" She looked at him with suspicion.

"There's a man in there by the name of Corey Robinson, he's wearing an expensive suit, and I recently saw him slip a date-rape drug into a woman's drink. I'm concerned he's going to do the same thing here."

"What? Why are you telling me? Why didn't you call the police?" she demanded, her expression betraying her anger and disgust.

"I'm working undercover, or I would have." He knew he should have handled the situation at Flannigan's differently, but it was too late now. "Please, do me a favor and keep an eye on him. I don't want anyone to get hurt. If you see him drugging a drink, call the police and let the woman know what's going on."

The bartender squinted at him through a haze of smoke, then dropped her cigarette and ground it under her heel. "Robinson? I think I know him. Older guy, paunchy and thinks he's hot stuff because he's rich."

"That's him," Hudd confirmed. "Thank you."

She nodded, brushed past him, and went back inside. Seconds later, she was behind the bar, smiling at Robinson. There was a young woman already seated beside him, and Hudd hoped and prayed that he wasn't too late. That her drink wasn't already drugged.

He slowly turned and climbed back into his Jeep. He decided to hang out and wait for a few minutes. He texted Kendra to let her know he'd be delayed. *Followed Robinson to Louisa's. Keeping an eye on him.*

Ok.

Hudd wished again he'd handled things differently. He could have confronted Robinson at Flannigan's, but he had been concerned that revealing himself would only result in his getting arrested for Jeanie's murder.

Which was still a strong possibility.

The minutes dragged by slowly. He wondered if Robinson had used up his allotment of whatever drug he had in Kendra's wine. Maybe the guy only carried enough for one drink, and when that was gone, he was done for the night.

Somehow, he didn't think Robinson was the type to give up so easily.

Thirty minutes went by before he heard the screech of a siren. A police cruiser came flying around the corner, red and blue lights flashing, and it abruptly stopped in front of Louisa's.

Two officers rushed inside. Through the long window, Hudd noticed that the bartender he'd spoken to was arguing with Robinson, holding on to his arm to keep him from leaving.

Hudd blew out a sigh of relief. Perfect. Robinson had been caught in the act. He started the Jeep and drove back toward the motel.

At least one problem was solved for the moment.

But he kept a keen eye out for cops as he took the lesser traveled highways back to Eagle. He didn't doubt Barkley had put the neighboring suburbs on notice about his arrest warrant. Which he felt certain had been issued.

He could only hope that Robinson's arrest would put a dent in Barkley's plan. It would have been nice to know what the two men discussed back at Barkley's house. And he wished he could find Nevins to see what he thought of his former classmates.

Hudd parked in the back of the motel near the dumpster again and performed a quick reconnaissance of the property to make sure the two detectives weren't sitting nearby waiting for him. After finding the area clear, he headed inside.

Kendra was sitting on the bed, her back against the headboard, her knees clutched to her chest. Before he could talk to her, though, Echo bounded through the connecting door to greet him.

"Hey, boy, how are you?" He gave the shepherd some well-deserved attention before glancing again at Kendra. "I need to take Echo outside, but you look pale. Are you okay?"

She grimaced and waved a hand at Echo. "I'm sick, upset, and angry, but there's nothing you can do to change that. Go take care of your dog."

Echo was already pushing past him to go out, leaving him little choice but to follow. After Echo took care of business, the animal was more than happy to come back inside.

"I'm sorry," Hudd said, even though he wasn't entirely sure what he was apologizing for.

She let out a harsh laugh. "You shouldn't apologize for saving me, Hudson. But I wish I could have punched Corey in the stomach. Hard."

He couldn't help but grin. "I would have loved to see that, but I want you to know you don't need to worry about him anymore."

She raked her fingers through her hair. "I wish I didn't have to, but I didn't get enough information out of him. I'll have to try again."

"No, you don't because he's been arrested."

His blunt statement had her jumping off the bed. "What are you talking about?"

He explained how he followed Robinson first to Barkley's house, then to Louisa's Lounge. "I told the bartender to be on alert, and I think she must have caught him spiking the drink because within thirty minutes a squad came barreling around the corner, and the two officers went inside."

"Good," she said, her expression fierce. "I never should have spilled my drink. I wish I'd confronted him and forced the wine to be tested."

"I know, and I'm sorry I didn't handle it better too." He lightly grasped her hand. "I was worried about blowing my cover, and I should have been more concerned about you."

"Don't be silly, I'd be in more danger if you blew your cover and managed to get arrested for Jeanie's murder." She closed her eyes for a moment. "I threw up, Hudson. I was so sick over what he intended to do to me that I puked at the side of the road."

He hated knowing she'd been that upset. He tugged her toward him. "I wanted to punch him too," he confided. "But I was afraid that once I started in on him, I wouldn't be able to stop."

A choked laugh emerged from her throat. Kendra rested her forehead on his chest, and he lightly held her in his arms, wishing there was something he could do to make her feel better.

"He's such an arrogant slimeball," she said, lifting her head to look at him. "I never imagined I'd say this, but Corey is far worse than my ex-husband, and he was pretty bad. But Don didn't have to drug women to sleep with him, they all trooped willingly into his bed."

"I'd say this is about Robinson needing to exert power over women. Forcing them to do what he wants is part of the thrill."

A shiver rippled over her. "He's disgusting. I hope he goes to jail for a really long time."

"Me too, but that may mean we're at a dead end when it comes to Zoey's murder," he pointed out. "If he's behind bars, then I doubt we'll ever know the truth about what happened twenty years ago, much less who killed Jeanie Mayberry."

"I know. I've done nothing but think about that while I was waiting for you." She pulled out of his arms. "I didn't learn much from Corey. I lied to him, mentioning how I saw David Nevins at the grocery store the night of Zoey's murder, and Corey went along with it. I can't figure out if that's because he wasn't really paying attention to who was there that night or if it was because he was the one missing from the party because he killed Zoey." Her dark gaze bored into his. "I want him to be guilty of murder, Hudson. I really do."

"I know." He glanced toward the connecting doorway. "Did you talk to Jamison about that night?"

"Not yet." She sighed. "I took a shower and brushed my teeth. We should probably grill him more about that night. Corey made it sound as if Jamison was there with the rest of the team."

"And Nevins was the only one Corey claimed wasn't there?" Hudson clarified.

"Yes. But only because I said I saw David at the grocery store."

Hudd nodded. He stared at her for a moment, then lightly kissed her cheek before heading into the next room. Echo followed as if understanding he was still on guard duty. The hour was just past nine o'clock, and he caught Joe Junior yawning when he came in.

"Hey, figured you guys would hit the sack by now," Hudd said with a smile.

"We—I was waiting for you." Jamison looked at him nervously.

"Let's chat for a few minutes, okay? Joey, keep an eye on Echo for me, would you?"

"Sure," the kid agreed.

"Tell us about the night Zoey was killed," Hudd said the moment they were out of the boy's earshot. "You guys were all at the party at Coach Donahue's house together, weren't you?"

"I wasn't," Jamison insisted.

"Corey Robinson said you were." Kendra stared at him. "Don't lie to me, Joe. Not about this."

"Look, I went to the party, sure. Why not? I was on the team too. But then Robinson showed up with two twelve-packs of beer. I thought for sure Coach Donahue would kick everyone out, but he laughed and claimed he was cool with it, didn't even seem to care if his own kid drank. Coach basically allowed them to pass the beer around. I hate beer, and I knew they would try to force me to have some, so I slipped out the back and left. I wasn't one of the popular kids, so I don't think they even noticed."

"But after Zoey's body was found, you claimed you were at the party?" Hudd asked.

Jamison hung his head. "Yeah. We all did."

"So how do you know that the threats weren't about the underage drinking rather than Zoey's murder?" Kendra asked in exasperation.

"Because they wouldn't threaten me over something as stupid as drinking, everyone did that back then. And Coach Donahue didn't care. It was no big deal," Jamison insisted. "I'm telling you, they were covering for Zoey's murderer."

Hudd believed him, but that wasn't enough. They needed actual proof.

"Was David Nevins there?" Kendra asked.

Jamison thought about that for a moment. "No, I don't remember seeing him there. But he could have showed up after I left."

"Okay, so you could have murdered Zoey. Or David could have," Kendra pointed out.

"I didn't. I had no reason to kill Zoey. She was always nice to me," Jamison protested.

Hudd shook his head with a frown. Everything about the night of Zoey's murder was shrouded in lies. At this point, he had no idea how they'd ever uncover the truth.

CHAPTER ELEVEN

For some reason, Kendra believed Joe's claim that he hadn't hurt Zoey. Not only did he lack motive, but he had been worried enough about his son to agree to Hudson's offer of protection. His fear of retaliation had been all too real.

Which brought them right back to Andrew and Corey. Specifically, Corey. The man deserved to rot in prison for the rest of his life, but she was very much afraid he'd find a way to weasel out of the charges. He was a slick lawyer accustomed to representing criminals. Bad guys, just like him.

A fresh wave of nausea swirled in her belly. Realizing how close she was to being a date-rape victim was frightening. Although she knew Hudson would never have let anything happen to her.

Thank goodness he'd insisted on being there tonight.

God had brought Hudson into her life for a reason. And she was immensely grateful for his strength and skill. He'd saved her life so many times over the past few days, she'd never be able to repay him.

Not that he'd want anything in return. Hudson was

honorable. He truly believed it was his job to keep her safe as they worked to uncover the truth.

"We need to get some sleep," Hudson said, breaking into her thoughts. "We'll need a plan to find Dave Nevins in the morning."

"I—uh, okay." Joe looked between them. "I figure the guys are all sleeping in one room?"

"Yes," Hudson's tone was firm. "Kendra deserves to have the privacy of her own room."

"Thanks." She tried to smile, secretly dreading being alone all night with her thoughts. Tempting to ask Hudson to stay with her. Inappropriate, but still tempting.

"I would ask that you keep the connecting door open," Hudson continued, eyeing her keenly. "If you don't mind."

"That's not a problem," she hastened to reassure him. "I'm still a bit unnerved about everything that happened tonight."

"Like what?" Joe asked.

Hudson quickly filled him in on how Corey had tried to drug her drink. Joe was appalled and relieved to learn Hudson had managed to alert the female bartender at Louisa's and have him arrested.

"I never liked him," Joe said. Then flushed when he glanced at her. "Sorry, Kendra. I know you dated him."

"I wish I hadn't, but I can't go back and change the past." It did make her wonder, though, if Corey had been doing that kind of thing back then. Or if this need to control women was something he'd developed over the years.

Joe returned to his room, leaving her alone with Hudson and Echo. He looked at her for a long moment. "Are you sure you're going to be okay?"

She forced a nod. "You saved me, Hudson," she said quietly. "I am so glad you're here."

"Me too." He smiled. "Get some rest. If you need me, I'm right next door."

"Okay." She turned away but then went back to hug him. "Thanks again," she murmured.

He pressed a kiss to the top of her head. "Anytime."

She held him for a long moment, then lifted up onto her tippy toes to kiss him. He returned her kiss but quickly broke away before things could get out of hand.

"Good night, Kendra."

"Good night."

She didn't sleep well. No surprise after everything that had happened, but Zoey's red journal flashed in her mind. They'd looked for it in the cave but hadn't found it. Was it possible the journal was hidden in the house Zoey grew up in? Or had her friend hidden it someplace else?

Most likely the diary had been found and destroyed years ago. She finally drifted off to sleep while wondering if there was a way to get inside Zoey's old bedroom.

The bright sunlight woke her the following morning. She squinted, putting a hand to her temple. She had a nagging headache, likely a combination of being dehydrated after her throwing-up episode combined with lack of sleep. She wished she had some sort of sports drink to sip to help stabilize her electrolytes.

Had there been a vending machine outside near the lobby? She rose, fished in her purse for a couple of dollars, then headed toward the door. The moment she stepped outside she saw Hudson with Echo.

She smiled as she watched them play. Echo leaped and jumped to Hudson's commands, and she marveled at the dog's agility. Hudson saw her and instantly came over to join her.

"Where are you going?"

"I want to check out the vending machine. See if they have a sports drink of some kind." She knew her headache was minor compared to what he'd suffered the other day. "I'm feeling dehydrated."

"Let's check it out."

She didn't think she needed a bodyguard to escort her to the vending machine, but she didn't argue. "I wish there was a way to get into Zoey's old bedroom. Finding her diary might be the key." She glanced over at him. "I can't help but think Corey tried something with her, only things got out of control, so he ended up strangling her to death."

"That's a possible theory," Hudson agreed. He stopped in front of the vending machine. "There's only one sports drink brand, do you want that one?"

"Yes." She pulled out her crumpled dollar bills and fed them into the machine. The bottle dropped into the tray. Hudson pulled it out and offered it to her. She downed a fourth of it, hoping she'd feel better soon.

"I don't think there's a way into Zoey's old bedroom," Hudson said. "So let's not go down that path. Besides, didn't you tell me how you guys always hung out down by the creek after school? Sounds like she tended to avoid going home."

"The trees." She mentally smacked herself upside the head. "I should have thought about searching the area around the trees. Maybe she buried the journal?" She frowned. "Would it be any good after all this time if she had?"

"Depends on whether or not she wrapped it up in plastic. Paper alone would disintegrate over twenty years, leaving nothing behind. But we all know plastic lasts forever."

"True." She couldn't help feeling a surge of excitement. "We need to check it out right away."

He nodded, gently steering her toward the motel room door. "We will, but in the meantime, we need to grab some breakfast. I'm sure Jamison and his son will be hungry."

She'd almost forgotten about the father-son team hiding in the adjoining room. "Of course. We'll go right after breakfast."

Hudson used his key to unlock the door. As they entered the room, she could hear Joe and his son arguing.

"I don't wanna sit here all day," Joey whined. "It's boring."

"Is it too much to ask for you to be safe?" Joe senior demanded. "One more day won't kill you."

"It might," Joey shot back defiantly.

Oh boy. She glanced at Hudson who grimaced. "I'll see what I can do," he said.

Kendra hoped that Corey's arrest meant Joe and his son were safe, but they wouldn't know that for sure unless they found some other evidence tying him to Zoey's murder. And to Jeanie's murder too.

As a trauma nurse, she knew very well that performing a toxicology screen was routine for all medical examiner's cases. If they found drugs in Jeanie's system, that may help implicate Corey in her murder.

The only problem with that was it took a good thirty days to get a tox screen back. At least in Portland. It was possible the Idaho state crime lab had a quicker turnaround. Or maybe a worse one.

She pulled out her phone and did a quick search. There was a phone number to call, but only during business hours. Still too early to call now.

The chance that they'd tell her anything was slim to

none. But maybe if she convinced them she was a concerned nurse who knew the victim, they'd at least give her a time frame for the tox screen to be completed.

Kendra couldn't deny the sense of urgency that plagued her. The detectives hadn't come to arrest Hudson, but she worried they'd pop up any minute to do just that.

They had to find something, and soon. The smashed bullet and cigarette butt weren't enough.

If they didn't? She'd beg Hudson to leave town. She'd feel much better if he disappeared into the mist. As a former SEAL, she felt certain he knew how to hide in a way the police would never find him.

"Okay, I think I've smoothed things over for now," Hudson said as he came through the connecting doorway. "Echo is going to stand guard while I head out to buy breakfast."

"No, let me go," she said. "I don't want you to be seen by anyone."

He arched a brow. "I know how to keep a low profile. Besides, I'm planning to use the drive-through."

She sensed arguing wouldn't get her anywhere. "I'll come with you, then."

"Fine." He shrugged and gestured to the door. "Let's go."

Grabbing the breakfast food didn't take long. Hitting the fast-food restaurant reminded her of her father, though, so she quickly called him. "Dad? How are you?"

"I'm fine, what did the surgeon say about your shoulder?"

She winced, wishing she didn't have to lie to him. "I—uh, haven't seen him yet. Still trying to get an appointment."

"You're a nurse, you should be able to get in ahead of the regular patients," he protested.

"That's not how it works, but don't worry, I'll be fine." She felt better hearing her father's voice. "I love you, Dad. Take care and I'll check in on you later."

"Okay, I love you too. Bye." Thankfully, her father hadn't sensed anything was wrong. He would have been horrified to know what Corey had tried to do the night before.

"I wish we could find out if Corey is still in jail." She glanced at Hudson as they drove back to the motel. "Too bad today is Friday, that means he'll get a chance to go before the judge to request bail."

"I know." Hudson took her hand in his. "Try not to worry about him. Even if he is released on bond, I'm sure he's going to keep a low profile. He won't risk doing something rash that will land him back in jail."

Logically, she knew he was right. But the idea of Corey being out of jail filled her with dread. The guy didn't deserve to be free, even for a short time.

She tried not to dwell on him. There were more important things to focus on. Like finding Zoey's journal.

And maybe talking to David Nevins. There had to be someone other than Joe Jamison who would be willing to talk about what had happened that Saturday night twenty years ago.

Hudson drove around the motel, making sure the police weren't nearby before he parked in the back next to the dumpster again. She followed him back to their rooms, the scent of the breakfast sandwiches making her realize how hungry she was.

"I'd like to say grace," she said after everyone had their meals. This time, Joe and his son didn't look surprised, and they politely bowed their heads. She caught Hudson's gaze and blushed when he smiled encouragingly. "Dear Lord, we thank You for providing us this delicious food and a safe place to stay. We ask for Your strength and guidance as we continue seeking the truth. Amen."

"Amen," Hudson echoed.

"Amen," Joe and his son said at the same time, making them laugh.

She took a bite of her egg sandwich, hoping and praying that today they'd find the truth they needed to keep Hudson out of jail.

Ironic to think the police wanted to arrest Hudson, the most courageous and honorable man she knew, while likely letting Corey the slime bucket out on bail.

Sometimes, the legal system was truly messed up.

HUDSON WORKED HARD to remain positive, even though he knew time was running out. If the police really wanted to find him, they'd start visiting all the motels. Maybe they'd even run a trace on his credit card, which was okay for now as he'd convinced the motel clerk to allow him to pay in cash by slipping him an extra hundred bucks.

Kendra believed they'd find Zoey's journal, but he doubted it was still around. He spent half the night trying to think of a way to talk to David Nevins without getting arrested for Jeanie's murder.

His only viable plan rested on Jamison making a call to Nevins requesting a meeting. They'd have to set something up in a neutral location while praying the cop would listen to reason before making a rash decision.

Corey Robinson's arrest had to work in their favor, right?

When they finished eating, Hudson drew Jamison aside. "I need you to call Nevins."

"Hold on," Kendra protested. She'd come up on his blind side without his noticing. "Don't call Nevins until after we check out the creek."

He turned to look at her. "Kendra, I know you believe Zoey had a diary, but spending our time digging around in the dirt on the off chance she buried it isn't the best use of our time."

"Zoey had a diary?" Jamison looked intrigued. "Are you sure?"

"Not one hundred percent certain," Kendra admitted. "But I remember her writing in a journal, and I think it's a possibility we can't afford to ignore." She paused, then added, "Zoey avoided going home after school. I've been thinking about that a lot and can't help but wonder if her brother's friendship with Corey was part of the reason she avoided going there."

Hudson knew Kendra believed Robinson was guilty of Zoey's and Jeanie's murders. Yet he wasn't convinced. "Okay, we'll look down by the creek for the diary. But I also want Jamison to reach out to Nevins. We need to know what, if anything, David remembers from the night Zoey died."

"What if he arrests you?" Kendra asked. "I'd rather we work on finding the diary than take that risk."

Hudd shrugged. "He might arrest me, but I'm hoping we can convince him that I'm innocent." He looked at Jamison. "Make the call."

"Okay." Jamison grimaced. "I'm not even sure he'll meet with me. The only reason I have his number is because of the reunion last year. He was pretty decent, talking to me and several of the other guys while Andrew, Corey, and Tristan acted like hot stuff."

The reunion he and Kendra hadn't attended. Strange that they were both here now, but he figured this must be part of God's plan. "Can't hurt to try," he assured Jamison. "Give it your best shot and make sure you act very concerned about your son's safety."

"I am," Jamison muttered as he pulled out his phone. "No need to put on an act."

He and Kendra were silent as Jamison made the call. Of course, Nevins didn't answer, so Joe left a message. "Dave, it's Joe Jamison. Look, I'd like to talk to you if you have time. It's about a threat made against my family. Please call when you have a chance, okay? Thanks." He lowered the phone and shrugged. "Hopefully he'll call back."

"You did good," Hudson assured him. "Let's head to the creek."

"What about Echo?" Kendra asked. "I know we want Joe and his son safe, but Echo might be able to help us find the diary."

She was putting a lot of faith in Echo, but Hudd couldn't blame her for wanting the additional protection. He looked at Jamison who nodded. "Go ahead, I think Joey and I are safe here."

He hesitated, then slowly nodded. "I think you should be fine here, especially with Corey's arrest and the fact that I paid for the room in cash. Call me if you need something, okay?"

Jamison glanced over his shoulder at Joey. "We will. The toughest job I'll face is keeping my son content."

Hudd clapped him on the back. "You'll be fine. And we won't be gone that long." He'd decided to give Kendra about an hour to find the diary before giving up on this idea and dragging her back here. He'd love to find a diary that exonerated him, but he wasn't holding his breath.

He hoped Robinson's arrest forced the DA's office to consider him a suspect in Jeanie's murder. And from there, maybe even link him to Zoey's murder too.

How long would Andrew Barkley cover for his buddy? Hopefully, the current chief of police would cut his losses, turning his back on Robinson to avoid being dragged into the mud with him.

Unless he was the one who killed his own sister.

The possibilities were endless, and he needed to stop spinning his wheels. He far preferred running ops as a SEAL. They were tasked with a mission, provided the necessary intel, and it was up to them to execute.

Far easier than trying to dig up twenty-year-old secrets.

"Are you ready?" Kendra tugged on his arm. "We need to get to the creek while it's early."

"I'm ready. Come, Echo." He headed for the door. "We'll need to stop and get a couple of small hand shovels."

"My dad has some in his garage," Kendra said. "Easier to stop there to pick them up."

He nodded, reluctantly agreeing with her plan. For one thing, they could get into the garage from the backyard. And secondly, they could avoid ending up on some store's security camera purchasing shovels.

They hurried out to his Jeep. Hudd put Echo in the back, glad to have his partner back. Then he drove toward Kendra's father's house, keeping a wary eye on the rearview mirror for an unwelcome tail.

Like the police.

He took the less-traveled side streets and pulled up along the house located directly behind Kendra's father's place. He turned to look at her. "Where are the shovels?"

"I'll grab them." She pushed open her car door and jumped down. "I'll be back soon."

Letting her go alone wasn't easy. If he had his way, she'd be back in Portland. But he told himself this wasn't nearly as dangerous as her meeting with Robinson.

Somehow it wasn't at all reassuring.

Drumming his fingers on the steering wheel, he silently counted the seconds in his head. After three minutes, he was ready to jump out of the Jeep to find her. Just then, Kendra emerged from between the houses carrying two small shovels.

She opened the back passenger door and set them on the floor. "Got them."

"Good." He blew out a breath. At this rate, he wouldn't need powder to gray his hair. Worrying about Kendra would do that for him.

The drive to the creek proved uneventful. They didn't pass a single squad, which made him wonder if his arrest warrant had been dropped. Since he couldn't plan on that, he decided to avoid the shack where he'd grown up.

He took the Jeep off-road, bouncing over the terrain until he found a spot where the vehicle couldn't be seen from the road. He killed the engine and turned toward Kendra. "We can't stay too long," he warned.

"I know." She hopped out and retrieved the shovels from the back seat. He took a few moments to get Echo out of the back before following her up and over the hill until they reached the cluster of trees.

It was the same spot where he'd stood three nights ago, watching Kendra as she stared out over the creek. Ironic how that brief meeting had turned into this, both of them working together to investigate Zoey's murder.

Granted, the shooter firing a round at them had spurred

that reluctant partnership. Yet he couldn't say he was sorry to be spending this time with Kendra.

He'd come to care about her. To the point he was seriously considering relocating to Portland, Oregon. A city he'd never even visited.

Not that she'd indicated she wanted him to do any such thing. But the thought wouldn't leave him alone. It didn't matter that he'd never been there. Any place Kendra lived was fine with him.

He pulled his thoughts to the present. To dream about the future meant he first had to settle the past. It was one thing to have Zoey's murder hanging over his head with people treating him as guilty, but Jeanie's murder changed everything.

"Okay, I think we should start here." Kendra waved toward the area in front of the trio of trees. "This is where we used to sit and do homework after school when the weather was nice."

He eyed the packed dirt. "Seems to me that someone might have noticed the dirt being disturbed if she'd really dug a hole here to hide her journal."

Kendra frowned. "I guess."

He moved around to the area behind the trees. There were scrubby bushes there, and he used his foot to push them to the side. The ground was packed down here, too, the result of twenty years of snow, sun, sleet, and rain, but he figured it was less likely anyone would have noticed the ground being dug up back here.

"Hand me one of those shovels."

Kendra gave him one. "I'll work on the front while you dig back here."

He nodded, secretly convinced they would both sweat

over this for nothing. He wedged the tip of the shovel into the dirt and leaned his weight on it.

The earth was rock solid. He could hear Kendra making grunting sounds as she tried to dig on the other side of the trees.

Echo wandered around the area, sniffing the ground. He was glad the dog hadn't growled or dug up any more cigarette butts.

It reminded him that he hadn't noticed Robinson smoking. The guy could have easily hired someone to shoot at him and Kendra, especially since he represented criminals as a defense lawyer.

Something to think about when it came time to talk with Nevins. The current cop and former army soldier was his best chance at getting answers. And if that didn't work? He tried not to go down that depressing path.

"This might not have been a good idea," Kendra said between grunts. "I'm barely making a dent out here. My shoulder is hampering my ability to dig."

"Take a break, let me see what I find here."

She muttered something he couldn't make out. His progress was going slightly better, and soon he had opened a hole about six inches deep and three feet wide.

"Hudson? Come here, quick!"

The urgency in Kendra's tone had him rushing to her side. She was sitting at the base of the trees, digging at a crevasse in the tree trunk.

"What are you doing?" He set the shovel aside and knelt beside her.

"I noticed the bark was loose on this tree, it looks like it's been infected with emerald ash borer. See?" She gestured toward the signature wavy lines on the trunk of the tree.

"Okay, so the tree will be dead soon." He wondered if

she was suffering from heat stroke despite the chill in the air. She needed more of that sports drink.

"No, that's not it. This, look here." She was prying her fingers into a deep groove of the tree. Then she picked up the shovel and used that to pry the wood away.

A glimpse of something blue caught his eye. "Let me help," he said, nudging her aside.

She moved away, and moments later, he pulled a blue collapsible lunch bag from the crevasse. He carefully opened it and saw there was a red notebook inside.

In that moment he realized Kendra had been right all along.

He could very well be holding the secret to who murdered Zoey in his hands.

CHAPTER TWELVE

Staring at Zoey's faded blue lunch bag containing the red notebook from twenty years ago was surreal. Kendra hoped she was right and that the pages weren't poems, the way Zoey had claimed.

"May I?" She held out her hand for the lunch bag. Hudson hesitated, then gave it to her.

She stared down at the notebook for a moment, then met Hudson's gaze. "Should I worry about fingerprints?"

"We should hand it directly over to the police," he admitted. But then he rummaged in his pocket. "I have small baggies to clean up after Echo, use these to protect your hands."

It was awkward but worked well enough. She drew out the notebook and carefully opened the first page. The paper had held up better than she could have hoped. Somehow the fabric collapsible lunch bag had preserved the notebook from the elements.

"Kendra, let's take the notebook with us and read it somewhere safer."

"Hold on, it might be nothing." She didn't move, her

gaze fixated on the page. The first page revealed Zoey's loopy handwriting. Memories of her best friend crashed over her, but she told herself to concentrate on what had been written.

After reading the first few sentences, she knew she'd been right. These were not poems but Zoey's somewhat meandering thought processes about her life, especially related to her father and brother.

They treat me like their maid, as if I'm only good enough to do their laundry and wash dishes. I hate them both!

"Well?" Hudson asked, breaking into her thoughts. "What does it say?"

"It's a diary of sorts, although she doesn't date and time the entries." She shrugged. "It's written as one long diatribe, although I can tell by the different inks that she added to it over time."

"Does it mention anything related to something one might kill her over?" Hudson asked.

"I haven't gotten that far."

"Let's go, we can read it later."

"Not yet. Give me a few minutes to see what I can find." She shared his impatience and tried to skim through the entries. It wasn't easy though because as she read Zoey's words, they would trigger memories. Some that she'd rather not relive, like the time they'd had a stupid fight over a deeply discounted dress that they'd both wanted. It was disheartening to realize how Kendra had gotten her way more often than not.

Finally, one sentence caught her attention, and she read it out loud. "I don't know what Kendra sees in Corey. He's a jerk."

"I agree," Hudson said dryly. "But does she go into detail as to why she thinks that?"

"I'm looking." She continued scanning the rambling script. Then her gaze caught another sentence. "My brother groped me in the bathroom. I thrust my knee in his nuts to escape."

"What?" Hudson came around to look at the notebook over her shoulder. "She really wrote that?"

"She did." A wave of nausea hit hard. "You don't think he . . ." She couldn't finish.

"I don't know." His tone was grim. "Keep reading."

She nodded, forcing herself to do just that. She found another statement related to Corey. "He cornered me after the pep rally and tried to kiss me. I managed to shove him away but haven't told Kendra yet. She probably wouldn't believe me anyway. Why would Corey be interested in me when he had her?" She shook her head. "Apparently, Corey always had the tendency to push women to do things they didn't want to do."

"Did he try that with you?" Hudson asked.

"Yeah, although he seemed to accept the boundaries I set. Which only makes me think that was why he pushed himself onto other girls. At least until the end of the school year where he made it clear he expected me to give him my virginity. That's when we broke up."

"That reminds me, did you smell cigarette smoke on Robinson last night? I was curious as to whether or not he smoked."

"No, and he didn't back in high school either." She grimaced. "I doubt he dropped the cigarette butt you and Echo found."

"Yeah, could be from anyone really." Hudson gestured to the notebook. "Both of those statements from Zoey make it clear both her brother and Robinson had reason to kill her. Especially if they continued to try to pressure her into doing something she didn't want to do."

"Maybe she'll tell us more." Kendra focused her attention back on the journal. "Here she talks about how you refused to go to homecoming and basically encouraged her to go with Tristan." She tipped her head to the side. "Why was that?"

"It was going to cost too much money, and I didn't want to hang out with people I didn't like," he said honestly. He shrugged, then added, "I knew my relationship with Zoey wasn't going anywhere. I told Barkley twenty years ago that I had no intention of going to homecoming or any other formal dance. This backs up my statement."

"It does." Another wave of shame hit hard. She'd treated Hudson so unfairly back then. They all had. She turned the page, grimacing when she saw it was the last one her friend had written. She read more slowly now, stopping at the last sentence. "I hate myself."

"Zoey said that?" Hudson asked with concern.

"Yes." She carefully set the notebook down on the lunch bag. "But she doesn't say why or name either Andrew or Corey as the reason she hated herself. I'm glad her death was ruled a homicide as this almost makes her seem suicidal."

Hudson looked disappointed, then used two more small baggies to protect his hands as he leafed through the notebook for himself. It didn't take long as Zoey hadn't written in the notebook every day. It seemed to Kendra as if her friend had used the notebook as a sounding board for bad events that had happened.

Rather than confiding in Kendra.

Guilt weighed heavily on her shoulders. She'd known

Zoey hadn't been happy, but she hadn't pushed her friend for details.

It hurt to know Kendra had failed Zoey in so many ways. The fact that Zoey didn't say her brother followed through with another attempt to abuse her or if Corey had tried again didn't mean those things hadn't happened.

In fact, she felt certain they had.

But that didn't help them identify which of the two men had murdered her.

"This is good evidence, Kendra, that we never would have found if not for your tenacity," Hudson said as he placed the journal back into the lunch bag. "I was hoping for more, but there's enough to indicate both her brother and Robinson should be considered viable suspects."

"I agree." She met Hudson's gaze. "Do we take it to the police station or call them to come out here? Do they need to see where it was hidden in the tree?"

"I'm not a cop, but I would think so. They'll want to photograph the spot that revealed the evidence." He glanced around, as if worried they were vulnerable out there. "I'd rather personally hand it to someone trustworthy. Maybe that includes David Nevins." He pulled his phone from his pocket. "Give me a minute to call Jamison. Maybe he's heard from Nevins by now. And if not, he should call him again. Especially now that we have this journal."

She nodded and listened as he made the call. Even though they were mostly hidden by the trees, she couldn't help but remember how the shooter had found them there before. She glanced nervously over her shoulder, scanning their surroundings. The only comfort she had was that Echo didn't appear concerned. He followed Hudson as he moved a few feet away to get better phone reception, his ears perked and his dark eyes alert.

No one would get close with Echo on guard.

Which didn't necessarily mean the shooter wasn't stationed someplace farther away.

"Good, we'll be here waiting," Hudson said with satisfaction as he returned to where she sat. "Thanks, Joe. You did good."

"David is coming to meet us?" she asked as Hudson pocketed his phone.

"Yes, in roughly twenty minutes. He wants to photograph the opening in the tree. Turns out Jamison was on the phone with Nevins when I called. He added me in so we could have a three-way conversation."

"That is good news." At least, she hoped David Nevins would treat Hudson fairly. Surely, after reading Zoey's journal, he would.

"David isn't working today," Hudson said. "But he agreed to meet anyway. And he confirmed there is a warrant out for my arrest."

"No!" She jumped to her feet. "Then we can't meet with him. As a cop, he'll have to take you in." She glanced around wildly. "You and Echo need to leave. Hide. I'll meet with David and give him Zoey's journal."

Hudson raised a hand. "I already told him I'd turn myself in."

"You can't!" She stared at him in horror. "Who is going to protect Joe and his son? And what about Echo? Please, Hudson, don't do this."

"They don't have enough evidence to hold me," he said. But a frown puckered his brow. "You're right about being safe, though. I'll need you to take Echo back to the motel and stay with Jamison until I'm released."

"Today is Friday, that may not be until Monday." She grabbed his arm and shook it. "Please hide, Hudson. I'll stay here and meet with David Nevins. I'll explain to him about how I saw Zoey writing in the journal and then dug around here until I was able to find it. I'm begging you not to turn yourself. Not today. Maybe on Monday, when you know you'll get to sit in front of a judge the following morning."

Indecision flashed across Hudson's features. "I told him I would, and I don't want to lie to a cop. Not when I'm already a suspect in two murders."

"But the most recent arrest warrant is primarily based on something that happened twenty years ago," she protested. "Don't you see? This is just Andrew Barkley's attempt to cover his tracks. We know now that he had a reason to kill his own sister. Maybe she threatened to go to their father or some other cop with what happened."

He blew out a heavy sigh and rubbed the back of his neck. She hoped another migraine wasn't brewing. "Here's what I'll do. I'll hide someplace nearby with Echo. Depending on how the conversation goes with Nevins, I'll either come out to talk to him personally or remain hidden until he leaves."

She scowled. "I'd rather you just stay hidden."

"I can't do that forever, Kendra. Besides, I told him I'd talk to him here. I don't like going back on my word. You have a good point about today being Friday, but the police could easily grab me later at the motel too. It's a risk I'll have to take."

"I have a better idea. You go pick up Joe and his son and take them to a new location while I meet with Dave." She stared him down. "That way you'll be safe until Monday."

"You are so beautiful when you're stubborn," Hudson said with a rueful smile. "I'm not leaving you until we know for sure we can trust Nevins. I'll be nearby, in case you need me."

She was stubborn? He was the one being incredibly obtuse. Being arrested was no joke. Granted, Hudson was now a respected former Navy SEAL rather than the troubled teen he was back when they were in high school, but she didn't trust Andrew Barkley as far as she could throw him.

Hudson turned, gestured for Echo to follow, and left through the brush, leaving her alone with Zoey's journal on the ground at her feet.

Reaching down, she grabbed it and wished for a safe place to hold on to it. It was too large to fit in her purse. Stuffing it beneath her sweater wouldn't work either. Obviously Nevins knew they had the journal, but she wasn't going to hand it over until she was good and ready.

She listened for Hudson and Echo, but she didn't hear anything. The man was the very definition of stealth. She believed he'd hide well enough not to be found unless David showed up with an entire cadre of cops.

Swallowing hard, she prayed that wouldn't happen.

The minutes ticked by with excruciating slowness. Standing here with Zoey's journal made her feel vulnerable. As if Andrew Barkley or Corey Robinson could walk up and tear it from her grasp, destroying it before she had a chance to turn it over to the police.

Please, Lord, protect me and the truth!

HUDSON STRETCHED out in a hollowed-out section of ground a few yards from the trees but located near more brush. He smeared dirt on his face, arms, and hair, then and settled in with Echo at his side to wait.

He didn't like lying to the police. He hoped his instincts

about Nevins were right and that the guy would listen to reason. If that was the case, Hudd would honor his promise by coming out and going in for questioning.

The only reason he'd agreed to hide for now was the idea of leaving Kendra and Jamison alone and vulnerable. Sure, they'd have Echo, but the dog couldn't stop a bullet.

He wanted to believe a fellow member of the armed forces had the integrity to do the right thing. But it wasn't as if all members of the military were honorable because he knew they weren't. He silently prayed trusting Nevins wasn't a mistake.

The sun beat relentlessly down on him, and he ignored the sweat dampening his temples. One thing was for sure, if he had to go into the police station, he'd need to call Kaleb or one of the other guys to come help him out.

Something he should have done earlier. He mentally cursed himself for being a dope.

He eased his phone from his pocket and quickly found Kaleb's number. Better late than never, right?

"Hudd? Is that you?" Kaleb's voice sounded unusually loud.

"Yeah, listen, I may need help. How long would it take you to get to Boise?"

"If I hop a plane, a few hours at most. I can rent a car once I get there if needed. What's going on?" Kaleb demanded.

"Long story." In the distance, Hudd could hear the sound of a car engine. Likely David Nevins. "I'll call you back later to let you know for sure, okay? I gotta go." He disconnected from the call.

To his credit, Kaleb didn't immediately try to call again, no doubt understanding Hudd was hiding out and couldn't talk. Just hearing Kaleb's voice was enough to calm Hudson's nerves.

He'd driven to LA to help Kaleb, only to find his swim buddy had everything under control by the time he'd gotten there. Kaleb must still be in the LA area with Charlotte, the woman he'd abruptly proposed to. The memory made him smile, but Hudd knew he should have considered hopping a plane to get to Kaleb. It was just second nature for him to remain alone.

"Officer Nevins? I'm Kendra Pickett."

"I remember you, Kendra. But where's Hudson Foster? He said he'd be here."

"I know he did, but you know as well as I do that he didn't kill anyone. Not Zoey twenty years ago and certainly not Jeanie Mayberry. I was with Hudson the night Jeanie was killed. And I found Zoey's journal in this nearly dead tree, which identifies two potential suspects, Andrew Barkley and Corey Robinson."

"You're sure it's hers?" There was interest in David's tone.

"Yes." From his vantage point, he could just barely see Kendra's jean-clad legs. "You know I was close friends with Zoey. We used to hang out here after school and in the summertime. I remembered her writing in a notebook and decided to see if I could find it. And I did."

"Does it have her name in it?" Nevins asked.

"No, but I recognize her handwriting," Kendra said firmly. "And I can verify that I saw her writing in the notebook several times. When I asked her what she was writing, she told me it was poetry. But it's not. In fact, it describes some despicable things she suffered at the hands of her brother, Andrew, and Corey Robinson."

Nevins didn't say anything for a long moment. "You'll

need hard evidence if your plan is to bring down the chief of police."

"Well, that won't be easy considering someone murdered Zoey before she could talk." Kendra's tone held an edge. "Thankfully, she documented what happened in this journal. I'm no legal expert, but I believe that's called motive, isn't it?"

From his position close to the ground, it wasn't easy to see what was happening. He lifted his head enough to see Nevins was looking around the area, no doubt trying to spot him.

And the guy was wearing his uniform.

Had he lied about being off duty? Or had he put on the uniform just so that he could arrest him?

Either way, Hudd didn't like it. It was the first indication that the soldier hadn't been honest with him.

"Do you mind if I take a look at the journal?" Nevins asked. "I'd also like to photograph the spot where you found it."

"If you use gloves. Zoey's fingerprints will likely be on the notebook, another way to prove it's hers."

"I planned on it," Nevins agreed.

"You were the one to find her body back then, right?" Kendra asked.

"Yeah. A group of us were searching this particular area, and I stumbled across the cave," Nevins admitted. "It was horrible to find her there."

The bushes that protected Hudd from view made it impossible for him to see anything other than their feet. He wished he could see Nevins's facial expressions to gauge his thoughts.

There was nothing but silence for several long moments. Hudd imagined Nevins reading through Zoey's personal thoughts and wondered what the guy would think of the statements she made about her brother and Robinson assaulting her.

"I know I was a lousy friend to Zoey," Kendra said in a low voice. "I feel terrible discovering what she went through. I really wish she would have confided in me, but she didn't. I didn't know any of this until today."

"Wow, this is very interesting," Nevins said. "It does raise a few questions about the investigation into Zoey's murder." Hudd watched as Nevins went over to the dead tree, likely to photograph the spot where they'd found the journal. Then the legs moved back toward Kendra.

"I totally agree. Do you mind if I ask you about the party Coach Donahue threw the night of her murder? Were you there?"

"No, unfortunately I was in the ER getting stitches in my hand from a dog bite," Nevins said. "I don't know if you remember, but we had a pit bull that we rescued. The dog went a little nuts and bit me one day. We ended up having to put him down."

"Oh, I think I do remember that." Kendra paused for a moment, then asked, "From what I hear, Coach Donahue allowed beer drinking that night."

"I heard about that the next day," Nevins said wryly. "Believe it or not, I was really upset to have missed it. I mean, hey, being allowed to drink beer at a party was a big deal back then."

"I guess." Kendra's voice held doubt. "I know Andrew and Corey were there, along with some of their teammates. I think it's possible they're covering for each other."

"Maybe." Nevins feet moved as if he were turning and scouring the area. "I'd really like to talk to Hudson."

"Why? Can't you see that Andrew and Corey set him

up on purpose? Do you know Corey was arrested last night in Boise?"

"What?" Nevins sounded surprised by that. "No, I didn't know he was arrested. For what?"

"Drugging a woman's drink at Louisa's Lounge," Kendra said. "I'm telling you, Hudson is innocent. The arrest warrant is a joke. I know he didn't hurt Zoey, her journal confirms his claim that he had no intention of going to homecoming, so he didn't kill her in a fit of rage that she'd decided to go with Tristan. Either Andrew or Corey killed her and they're covering for each other. Joe Jamison will confirm that part."

There was another long silence as Nevins seemed to digest what Kendra was telling him. Hudd found himself holding his breath. If Nevins agreed with her, he'd risk coming out to talk to the guy.

But if he didn't, maybe he'd hold off for a bit. It couldn't hurt to wait until Monday to turn himself in.

Hudd heard the rustle of plastic, then the click of a lighter. His entire body tensed when he was hit by the scent of cigarette smoke.

He quickly reached over to close his hand around Echo's snout and gave the hand signal for quiet so the dog didn't begin to growl, giving away their location.

In that moment, he feared the worst. That David Nevins was the shooter, hired by either Barkley or Robinson to shut them both up.

Permanently.

CHAPTER THIRTEEN

Kendra took a hasty step back when David pulled out a pack of cigarettes, shook one loose, and lit up. All she could think of was the butt that Hudson and Echo had found not far from the shack.

Had they gotten it wrong? Was Nevins involved in this?

"Are you going to call your boss about the journal?" She strove to sound calm and casual. "It's important evidence in an open homicide case."

David nodded. "Yeah, for sure this has to be logged in as evidence. But where is Hudson? He said he was turning himself in."

She prayed that Hudson would remain hidden, although being alone with David made her feel vulnerable. David hadn't reached for his weapon, which was good, but the moment he did, she was toast. There's no way she'd be able to escape.

Still, she took another subtle step backward, putting more distance between her and David. Hudson was armed with a gun and a knife. A fact that had frightened her the first time they'd met right here in this spot but was now extremely reassuring.

"Look, Hudson didn't kill Zoey or Jeanie. If he turns himself in today, he'll end up sitting in jail all weekend. He told me to let you know he'd turn himself in on Monday."

David squinted at her through a cloud of smoke. "That wasn't the deal."

"What would you do if you were falsely accused of murder?" she shot back. "Zoey's journal proves her brother and Corey Robinson both had more reason to harm her than Hudson did. Don't you see? He's being set up to take the fall."

David sighed and shook his head. "I hear what you're saying, Kendra. I do. But I can't go against the chief of police. And when Barkley issues an arrest warrant, he expects us to follow through."

"Oh, sure, don't rock the boat." She didn't bother to hide her sarcasm. "Why worry about a pesky thing called the truth? Is that how you functioned in the army too?"

He looked surprised. "How did you know I served?"

"Research," she responded. "Did you know Hudson served twenty years as a Navy SEAL?"

David dropped the cigarette and ground it beneath his boot heel. His hand went to his weapon.

Out of nowhere, Hudson rushed toward the cop, his face and hair covered with dirt, his expression fierce. Echo let out a series of loud, sharp staccato barks that reverberated through the air. Kendra instinctively ducked behind the trio of trees as Hudson took David to the ground.

"You're assaulting a cop!" David said in a hoarse voice. His face turned red as Hudson leaned his forearm against the guy's windpipe.

"You went for your gun." Hudson glared at him. "Who's paying you? Barkley or Robinson?"

"I—don't know what you mean?" David bucked beneath Hudson, trying to break free. "I'll arrest you for this, Foster."

"Not if no one finds your body." Hudson glanced at Echo who was still barking like a maniac. "Sit, Echo. Stay. Guard."

Echo sat, panting over David's face.

Kendra came out from behind the trees, bending down to look at the cigarette butt David had crushed beneath his heel. "Hudson? I'm not sure this is the same brand you and Echo found the other day."

Hudson removed David's weapon from its holster, then divested the cop of his Taser, baton, and cuffs. "Come get these, Kendra. Keep them far out of his reach."

She hurried over to gather the items, being extra careful with the gun. She knew nothing about firearms, other than how to treat the end result when bullets ripped through tissue, muscle, and bone.

"Got them," she said breathlessly.

"Good." Hudson leaned back and then hauled David to his feet. "Give me the handcuffs, then put the rest of his stuff behind the trees."

"You'll pay for this, Foster." David's face was red with anger as Hudson cuffed his hands behind his back.

"Why did you reach for your gun, Nevins?" Hudson asked calmly. "And don't try to hurt me, Echo is very protective."

David looked nervously at the shepherd. "I didn't. It's just a habit to rest my hand on my gun."

"And maybe it's just a habit to shoot at innocent people, like Kendra."

David glanced at her, then back at Hudson. "I didn't shoot anyone! Why would you think I did?"

"You left a cigarette butt in your hidey hole the other day," Hudson drawled. "You tried to bury it, but Echo found it."

"What hidey hole?" David was clearly getting frustrated. "I don't know what you're talking about."

Kendra stepped forward and picked up the cigarette butt he'd dropped. "Hudson, look. The butt on this one is white, not tan like the one you found."

"I'm trying to quit," David muttered. Then he narrowed his gaze. "You really attacked me because of a cigarette butt?"

"Because you went for your weapon," Hudson corrected calmly. "And because I don't trust you. Maybe you buy whatever cigarette brand that happens to be on sale. The different-colored butt doesn't sway me from believing you may have shot at Kendra not once but twice. And tried to run her off the road."

"You're losing it, Foster," David said wearily. "I'm not the bad guy here."

Kendra stepped up to put a hand on Hudson's arm. "You need to take Echo and get away. Clearly this isn't the time to turn yourself in."

"We'll both go," Hudson said. "The only question is what to do with Zoey's journal. I'm not sure who we can trust with it."

She wasn't sure what to do with the notebook either. She'd hoped David would prove to be one of the good guys. And maybe he was.

But there was a chance he wasn't.

"Hold on, Foster. You can't leave me here cuffed and unable to defend myself," David complained.

Hudson stared at him. "Where's your partner? Why did you come here alone, in uniform on a day you said you were off duty?"

David flushed. "Okay, I lied. I'm not off duty today, I'm working. I figured you'd be more comfortable hearing I was off duty than on. But that doesn't mean I'm guilty of shooting at Kendra. That's crazy. Why would she be in danger anyway?"

"Because I've been asking questions about Zoey's murder." She glared at him. "I told the police officer on duty shortly after I came home that I planned to find evidence to put the real killer away."

David's gaze dropped to the notebook in her arms. "And you did." He seemed to realize what had been happening. "You're really in danger."

"Ya think?" Kendra gestured toward Hudson. "He's the only reason I'm still alive. There have been several attempts to kill me and an attempt to drug me. I thought for sure you were going to shoot me."

David blew out a long breath. "Okay, I get it. I swear I'm not the bad guy here. I like my job, but to be honest, Chief Barkley is a jerk. No way would I risk breaking the law for him, no matter how much money he offered."

Kendra wanted to believe him. She glanced at Hudson who was staring at David intently. "You always ride alone?"

"We do, yes," David confirmed. "Thanks to the budget cutbacks put in place by Barkley. This isn't New York City or Los Angeles. The recent murder of Jeanie Mayberry is the first homicide in three years. According to the chief, we're not in danger the way cops are in big cities."

"Stupid," Hudson muttered.

"Hey, I agree. Although, to be honest, I feel much safer here than I did in the army." David's expression turned grim. "Until now. You came out of nowhere and flattened me before I knew what was happening. Time to take the cuffs off, Foster. I won't press assault charges if you release me."

Hudson ignored him and turned toward her. "I have an idea about where to take the journal."

"Where?" She glanced nervously at David. "Another cop?"

"No, the newspapers. We'll meet with a reporter and get the contents of the journal out in the open. From there, we can talk to the FBI."

"That's a good idea," David agreed. "The Feds have gone in to clean up corrupt police stations. They'll take Zoey's journal seriously."

"Okay, I like the idea of going to the FBI," she admitted. "But we need to let David go. I don't want you facing any more charges. The current arrest warrant is bad enough."

Hudson looked thoughtful for a moment. "Okay, I have a plan. Echo, guard." He turned to Kendra. "Stay here while I get the Jeep."

"Okay." She wasn't afraid to stay with David now that he wasn't armed and with Echo on guard. Yet she was feeling a bit guilty. "I'm sorry if you're truly innocent, David. But you have to understand how much danger we're in. It's difficult to trust anyone right now, and that unfortunately includes you."

"So much for cops getting the respect they deserve," David said bitterly.

"You read what Zoey wrote about Andrew," she reminded him. "Does he deserve respect?"

David fell silent for several seconds before shaking his head. "I guess not. But I didn't shoot at you, Kendra. I didn't kill Zoey or Jeanie either."

"I want to believe you," she said. "But at this point, we can't take the risk."

The rumble of the Jeep's engine reached her ears. She waited as Hudson drove over the rocky terrain toward her. She could tell David was surprised and chagrined that he hadn't checked the place out thoroughly enough.

She'd trust Hudson's instincts over anyone else's every day of the week.

He stopped the Jeep and hopped out. He opened the back hatch and made a gesture with his hand hitting the center of his chest. "Come, Echo."

The German shepherd eagerly abandoned his guard duty, gracefully jumping into the back. Kendra gave David a rueful smile as she went over to get into the passenger seat, bringing Zoey's journal with her.

Hudson stood in front of David for a long moment. "If you're one of the good guys, then I'm sorry. But I won't put Kendra in danger." He pulled something from his pocket and tossed it toward the thick brush behind the trees. "That's the key to the cuffs. You should be able to get free before too long."

Kendra was surprised that David didn't protest or say anything else. He simply watched as Hudson climbed behind the wheel, put the Jeep into gear, and headed off.

Turning in her seat, she watched through the rear window as David went over to peer down at the ground, searching for the handcuff key within the brush. She turned back and sighed. "I doubt he's involved."

"No way to know for sure," Hudson said grimly. "We need to call Jamison, though, to warn him."

"Yeah." She felt exhausted, even though nothing had really happened. She frowned when she noticed Hudson's pained expression. "What's wrong?"

"Headache," he said curtly. "Came on when I hit the ground."

She winced and quickly pulled out her phone to call Joe. Just when she thought things couldn't get any worse, Hudson was coming down with a migraine. They needed to get someplace safe before Hudson became incapacitated.

When she pushed the button to call Joe, his phone went straight to voice mail. She frowned and tried again.

Still nothing.

She sent a text message, asking him to call her back, but received no response.

"What is it?" Hudson asked.

"Joe's not answering, his phone went straight to voice mail. I tried a text message too."

Hudson grimaced but didn't say anything. He lowered the visor to blunt the bright sunlight streaming in.

"Pull over, Hudson, let me drive. You should try that pressure point release trick I showed you."

"I'm fine. Keep trying Jamison." There was a rough edge to his tone as if he were hanging on by a thread.

Kendra prayed they'd find Joe and his son unharmed and in time to get them someplace safe before Hudson succumbed to the debilitating pain.

HUDSON GRITTED his teeth and tried to ignore the pounding in his temple. He didn't have time for this. He knew that the minute Nevins got free of his cuffs, he'd be on the radio sending squads on their tail. Nevins was smart enough to put a BOLO out on his Jeep.

The only mitigating factor he'd been able to come up with was to use water from the creek to smear mud over his license plate. That alone could get him pulled over, but considering the rest of his Jeep was splattered with mud, he hoped it wouldn't catch anyone's attention.

He knew he was living on borrowed time. It was highly unlikely he'd make it through the rest of the day without getting arrested.

There had to be a way to ensure Kendra's safety before that happened.

"Still no answer from Joe," she said.

"Look up the address of the FBI office in Boise," he instructed. "There isn't time to deal with the reporters. We'll have to take our chances with the Feds."

"Are you sure?" Kendra asked.

"I'm worried about Joe and his son." Hudson was kicking himself for not leaving Echo behind to protect them. Although if the police had gone there, one of the cops may have shot the dog.

Still, knowing Joey might be in danger troubled him. The kid was only ten, he didn't deserve to be put in this position.

Kendra rattled off the address of the FBI office. "You think they'll take our concerns seriously?"

"I hope so." He blinked, willing the headache to go away. His vision was beginning to blur, not a good sign.

"Hudson? Maybe you should pull over." Kendra's voice sounded as if it were coming from the end of a long tunnel.

He forced himself to keep driving, desperately searching for a place to go temporarily. He abruptly turned into a park, driving through the winding roads until he found a secluded spot.

"Good idea, I'll take over from here."

He backed the Jeep into an alcove between two large

trees. Unfortunately only one was an evergreen, the other had bare branches as spring had barely sprung.

It was the best he could do. He shut down the Jeep, then slumped against the driver's side door, gratefully closing his eyes. He may have heard Kendra talking, but the sounds were garbled and made no sense.

His head felt like it was on fire. He tried to pull himself into a ball to avoid being scorched by the flames.

Hudd had no idea how long he battled the intense headache. He thought he felt Kendra's fingers on his scalp, but he was distracted by images of his last mission flashing in his mind. It was the moment he'd been struck by the bomb fragment moments after he'd noticed Jaydon going limp in the water beside him. As always, he battled the ocean, trying to get to his teammate, his lungs so tight he knew it was only a matter of time before they exploded right out of his chest. Then he finally broke free of the ocean's grip, reaching the surface and gasping for breath.

The nightmare combined with the pain reverberating through his head lasted for what seemed like hours. Finally, the pain receded enough for him to lift his head. Seeing the trees and the road in front of him was confusing. For a moment, he had absolutely no idea where he was.

Then he remembered driving through the park. He glanced over, concerned to see Kendra wasn't in the passenger seat.

Panic gripped him around the throat. Had she been kidnapped while he was out? But then he realized Echo wasn't in the back either.

Swallowing a groan, he sat up straighter and pushed at his driver's side door. It didn't budge because he had the strength of a gnat.

"Come on, Hudd," he whispered. He pulled the handle

and used his shoulder to ram the door open. The cool air felt good against his features, and he realized he was damp with sweat that had smeared with the dirt covering him.

"Hudson? Wait. Are you okay?" Kendra hurried toward him, and he momentarily closed his eyes to thank God she was unharmed. Echo came over to nudge him. He reached out to stroke Echo's fur, glad Kendra had taken care of him.

"How long was I out?" He forced the words past his dry throat.

"Ninety minutes." Her gaze was full of concern as she checked him over. "I used the pressure points on your scalp, but it didn't seem to work as well. Although you seemed to come out of this attack faster than last time."

An hour and a half was bad enough, but he knew she was right. At some level he had felt her fingers helping to ease the pressure. He owed her a debt of gratitude. "Have you heard from Jamison?"

"No, I made a quick call to the ME's office, but they wouldn't tell me anything about Jeanie's murder or the contents of her tox screen. Then I turned my phone off because I wanted to preserve the battery." She pulled the device from her pocket. "I also didn't want to bother you."

"I doubt I'd have noticed," he said wryly. "We need to get to the FBI office ASAP."

The moment Kendra turned her phone on, it rang. She quickly hit the speaker button. "Joe? Are you and Joey okay?"

"Uh, yeah, but the cops are here. They want to talk to you and Hudson." Jamison's tone was strained.

Hudson shook his head, wincing as the motion made tiny stars float into his line of vision. "No," he whispered in a voice he hoped only she could hear.

"Sorry, Joe, but I have to go." She disconnected from the

call. "Now what?"

Instantly, her phone rang again. She silenced the call and then turned the device off again. "Keep it off," he told her. "Do you remember the address of the FBI office?"

"I do. It's on Main Street, but maybe we should head over to the restrooms first." She waved a hand. "You might want to clean up a bit."

She was right. Besides, he needed some water. His mouth was gritty with dirt. "Are they close?"

"Yes, I just came from there." She waved at a barely there path. "Just head through the woods, and you'll find them on the other side of the small hill."

"Stay here with Echo." He staggered in the direction she'd indicated. Another thirty minutes of downtime would have been nice, but he told himself to get over it. He'd already wasted ninety minutes, and the police had found Jamison and his son at the motel.

It wouldn't take them long to find him either.

He mentally cursed his weakness in succumbing to the migraine. Not that he'd had much choice in the matter. Still, he hated feeling weak and helpless. Thank goodness Kendra had been able to shorten the time he was down.

Having Zoey's journal was their golden ticket to convince the Feds to look into their case. Before that, it would have been his word and Kendra's against the current chief of police and a current defense lawyer. They may have been more believable after Robinson's arrest, if the charges manage to stick to the guy, but at this point, Barkley had his career and that of his father to back him up.

He washed his hands, then cupped them beneath the faucet and drank several mouthfuls of water. Hudd knew he was dehydrated, but there wasn't a vending machine here the way there had been at the motel. After drinking his fill, he washed up his face and arms the best he could. There was still dirt embedded in his hair, but staring at his image in the mirror, he decided it was the best he could do.

A keen sense of urgency had him hurrying back to the Jeep. He relaxed when he noticed Echo was in the back crate area and Kendra was behind the wheel. He hesitated, then decided to let her drive. As much as he hated to admit it, he wasn't at his best. His muscles felt like limp spaghetti.

This new normal of experiencing these migraines attack at the most inconvenient times was difficult to get used to. That and trying to see what was happening around him with only one eye. Thankfully, he had Echo to help support him.

Kendra too.

He climbed into the passenger seat.

"You look much better." She smiled as she started the engine. "We'll stop along the way to grab some water."

"Not necessary." His voice still sounded raspy as if sore from screaming through his nightmare. "I'm fine. Let's just get this journal to the Feds." He wished he hadn't gone down the path of trusting Nevins, but he had chosen instead to head straight to the FBI. Better yet, he should have called Kaleb, Mason, or any of his teammates for help earlier instead of taking on the role of the Lone Ranger. Even if he called Kaleb now, it would take too long for him to be of help.

Knowing ninety minutes passed since they'd left Nevins was concerning. It wouldn't have taken the cop and former soldier very long to get free of the cuffs once he'd found the key he'd been stupid enough to leave behind.

No doubt, Nevins tried to find his Jeep first, then had tracked down Jamison and his son. At least they were both okay. For now. He wanted to believe Nevins wouldn't hurt a man and his son. But it was clear that Chief Barkley called the shots. And he hated to think about what might happen after Barkley learned Jamison had spoken to him and Kendra.

If anything happened to the boy, Hudson wouldn't be able to forgive himself.

Exhaustion weighed heavily on his shoulders. Between their precarious position, knowing Joey and his father might be in danger, and the remnants of his migraine, he needed every ounce of strength to remain upright.

Sleep wasn't an option, so he forced himself to keep a wary eye out for cops as Kendra drove through the park.

"Stay on the back roads," he advised. "Hopefully once we hit downtown Boise, we won't have to worry so much."

"I hope Joe and his son are okay," she said, glancing at him. "I really wanted to believe that David wasn't a part of this."

"I know. He may be innocent, but I wasn't willing to risk your life on that fact. He seemed glad to hear we were going to the FBI."

"What if he goes there to meet up with us?"

"Just get us to downtown Boise," Hudd said wearily. "Once we get there, I'll do some recon to check the place out. If Nevins is in the area, we'll go to plan B."

"And what does that entail?"

He considered their options. Going to a reporter was one way to get their story out there, but time was of the essence, and they needed the support of the federal government. "We can keep driving, head to Portland, Oregon. I'm sure there are FBI offices there."

"Okay, that sounds good." She continued maneuvering through traffic.

Within five minutes, he caught a glimpse of a squad

behind them. His heart sank, although at this point, the driver hadn't yet hit his lights and sirens. "Kendra, there's a cop behind us."

"I see him." Her voice was tight, and she glanced at him nervously. "What should I do?"

"Stay calm but try to lose him." Hudd had a bad feeling about this. He pulled his Sig Sauer from the belt holster.

"What are you doing? You can't shoot at a cop!"

"I won't shoot to kill, just to disable the vehicle." He twisted in his seat to get a better view out the back window as his left side was his blind eye.

Kendra abruptly sped up a bit in time to make a green left turn signal. He braced himself with a hand on the dash as he watched their six.

The squad was no longer visible. Yet he wasn't reassured. If the driver had been tailing them, he could easily use his radio to call another squad in to help track them down.

Kendra was whispering something as she drove. He felt bad when he realized she was praying for safety.

"We're going to be okay," he assured her. "The worst they can do is arrest me, Kendra. It's not the end of the world."

"What if Andrew sends someone to kill you while you're behind bars?" She darted a glance at him, then concentrated on driving.

"Okay, first of all, you've been watching too many police shows," he said dryly. "And second, I'm a trained Navy SEAL. You have to trust me when I say I can take care of myself, even behind bars."

"That's just it, you're innocent, Hudson. You shouldn't have to defend yourself while being in police custody," she protested.

"Don't worry about me," he repeated. "Look, we're only a few miles from downtown Boise. We'll be at the FBI office before you know it."

She gave a curt nod. A few minutes later, she said, "Tell me where you'd like me to drop you off."

He checked the billboards and other signs for hints on where they may be able to stop without drawing too much attention. "Is that a grocery store?"

"Yes. I think it's only a few blocks from the building." She pulled into the parking lot, choosing to park the Jeep between a van and a large, oversized pickup truck. "Be careful, Hudson."

"I will." He slid out and lightly shut the door. Then he went around the back of the grocery store to come up on the other side of the street.

He recognized the area from following Robinson the night before. He continued moving toward the federal building, his gaze narrowing as he drew close enough to see there were two squads parked out front and one sitting along the adjacent road.

Not good. Nevins had put the Boise police on alert.

He immediately detoured into a small fast-food restaurant. After purchasing two bottles of water, he left through the door near the restrooms.

Still moving casually as to not draw attention, he made it back to the Jeep. Kendra's eyes widened when she saw him returning so quickly.

"Time to enact plan B," he said curtly.

"Dear Lord, guide us to safety," she whispered. Then she backed the Jeep out of the parking lot and headed off in the opposite direction of the FBI offices.

Hudd hoped this worked because if it didn't, he was fresh out of ideas.

CHAPTER FOURTEEN

Kendra gripped the steering wheel tightly as she navigated the streets of downtown Boise. Thankfully, it wasn't a huge metropolis, but that only made it easier for the cops to spot them.

She glanced at Hudson. "Maybe we should go back to get my car. I know it's red, but David probably told them we were in your blue Jeep."

"Too risky to head back to the motel." He scowled. "And Echo is safer in the back of the Jeep. We could rent a car, but that would take time. Right now, they're still waiting for us to show up at the FBI office. Hopefully, we'll be halfway to Portland before they catch on."

"Okay." She couldn't argue his logic. Although she was concerned that the cops, especially Andrew, would assume her place of residence being in Portland would be their next stop. "I wonder if we shouldn't head down to Salt Lake City instead. It's roughly a five-hour drive, give or take a few minutes, and that's a good ninety minutes less than it would take to reach Portland."

"Good idea," Hudson agreed. "Let's do that. But we

both need to be on alert for cops. I have no doubt that Barkley and Nevins have given the state police a heads-up to be looking for my Jeep."

"I know." She felt better, having a decent plan to escape detection. Going to Salt Lake City, Utah, meant driving longer through the state of Idaho, but that didn't worry her as much as she knew the area was very rural. Mountain Home was a decent-sized city, and after that, the next largest they'd reach was Twin Falls. Her parents had taken her to Twin Falls when she was thirteen, and she had fond memories of the breathtaking scenery. It was one of many places she'd hoped to share with her daughter, Olivia, when she was old enough.

But Olivia had been called home by God. Tears misted in her eyes. She quickly swiped them away.

*Don't go the*re, she warned herself. She couldn't afford to become an emotional wreck right now.

Not when they couldn't even trust the police to keep them safe.

She glanced at Zoey's journal tucked between the seat and the center console, hoping and praying the FBI would consider the words her former friend had written along with the attempts against her and Hudson as enough evidence to open an investigation into Andrew Barkley. If there was ever a cop who deserved to be scrutinized, it was Andrew.

"Do you think Corey has gotten out of jail?"

"Probably. He knows how to work the legal system, and I'm sure he also knows the judges by name."

"I wonder if Zoey's journal would help the DA's office in pressing charges against him." The way he'd drugged her drink still bothered her. Knowing he was sick enough to have done that to other women was enough to make her want to kick him the way Zoey had kicked her brother all those years ago.

"I'm not an expert, but I don't think the judge will allow prior bad acts to come in as evidence, especially when the action took place twenty years ago." He lightly touched her arm. "However, you and I can testify against him for what he tried to do back at Flannigan's. Once we know we're safe," he added.

"I know. I just wish I'd saved some of the wine he'd drugged." She shook her head. "I should have made sure some of the liquid landed on me. Maybe they still could have tested the contents."

"Doubtful," Hudson said. "Try not to stress about Robinson. He'll get what he deserves. Especially if we can prove he murdered Zoey and Jeanie."

She nodded. "Uh, we probably need to fill up with gas soon. We have less than a quarter tank, and the lower part of the state is fairly desolate."

"Okay, I just saw a sign for a gas station up ahead. It's right off the interstate. Let's fill up now so we don't have to worry. I'd like to let Echo out too."

"We should stock up on some food and water. The next gas station is likely a couple of hours away." She made it sound like they were taking a recreational road trip when it was anything but. If they weren't trying to avoid the local cops long enough to speak to the FBI, this foray across the state might be enjoyable.

Instead, she was tense and jittery, expecting a squad to pop out of nowhere with lights flashing and sirens blaring to pull them over.

Two miles later, she exited the interstate to pull into the gas station. There was a small convenience store attached, stocked with overpriced items.

Hudson took care of letting Echo out to do his business while he filled the Jeep with gas. She headed inside to use the restroom, then to search for something to eat.

Their day had started early, and it was going on eleven thirty. They really needed to grab something while they had the chance.

Her gaze landed on the *Idaho Statesman* newspaper. She picked it up and scanned the headlines, hoping there may be something about Corey's arrest.

"Hey, are you planning to buy that?" A crotchety man behind the counter scowled at her. "Can't just read it for free. Costs a dollar fifty."

"I understand, and yes, I'll buy it." She tucked the folded up newspaper under her arm and went back to pursuing the shelves and coolers for food. Hudson joined her a few minutes later with Echo at his side. Thankfully, the crabby old man didn't seem to care about the dog being inside the store.

"We should hurry," he said in a low voice. "The faster we get to Salt Lake City, the better."

This constantly dodging the police was exhausting. She grabbed a premade sandwich from the cooler along with a large bottle of water. Hudson did the same and insisted on paying as they checked out. When he pulled cash from his pocket, it made her realize that he was trying to avoid using his credit card.

"Let's go." He ushered her toward the Jeep, going around back to let Echo in. "I'll drive for a while."

"I can do it," she protested, but he ignored her. With a sigh, she climbed into the passenger seat. Having him drive would give her time to read the newspaper.

Hudson started the engine, then muttered something harsh under his breath.

"What happened?" As soon as the words left her mouth, she saw the state police cruiser slowly coming down the interstate exit ramp. Her heart pounded painfully in her chest as Hudson wrenched the wheel and drove around to the back of the gas station. He didn't hesitate to go up and over the curb to find a better hiding spot.

He killed the engine. "Stay here while I check things out."

"Wait! Don't leave. There's no reason for him to look back here, is there?" She hated the idea of sitting there alone while he put himself in danger. Especially since he was the one with the outstanding arrest warrant.

"Trust me," Hudson said simply.

"I do." She trusted him more than she'd ever trusted any other man, except maybe for her father. Certainly, her taste in men was sorely lacking, proven by how she'd dated a horrible man like Corey in high school, then by marrying her cheating ex-husband. It was humbling to realize that she knew deep in her soul Hudson would never do either of those things.

She released his arm. "Just—be careful."

He smiled, then slid out from behind the wheel. She watched as he moved stealthily along the side of the building. Then he disappeared around the corner.

"He's going to be fine, Echo," she said when the dog pawed at the side of the Jeep. The shepherd clearly wanted to go with Hudson. "He'll be back soon."

After a solid fifteen minutes, Hudson returned. He opened the driver's side door and slid in behind the wheel. "All clear. He's gone."

"So he wasn't looking for us."

Hudson shrugged. "It didn't appear that way. He filled up with gas, disappeared inside the store. He took his sweet time using the restroom and whatnot, then left. But I think we should stay here for a few more minutes, just to make sure we don't run into him on the interstate."

"Okay." She managed a weak smile. "I bought the paper to see if there's anything about Corey's arrest. You would think a well-known lawyer being accused of drugging women with date-rape drugs would make the front page."

"You would," he agreed.

She unfolded the newspaper and scanned the headlines. Nothing on the first page, of course, so she moved on.

Nothing on the second and third pages either.

"I can't believe it," she said, her stomach tightening. "I don't see anything mentioned about Corey's arrest."

Hudson frowned. "I know I saw the squad pull up to the lounge," he said. "And the bartender had Corey's arm."

A cold finger of dread snaked down her spine. "What if Corey managed to place the blame on someone else?"

"Does the newspaper mention any other arrests."

She read through the headlines again, being careful not to skip any. Then she lowered the newspaper. "Nothing. You know what this means? It's Friday, heading into a weekend. Corey could be already planning to find his next victim."

"Or it could be that the news of his arrest didn't make the paper yet," Hudson said calmly. "Don't panic. Let's stay focused on talking with the FBI. Once we have them on alert to what's going on, we'll find out what happened with Robinson."

"Okay." She tried to relax her tense muscles, but it wasn't easy. Every cell in her body was repulsed by the idea of Corey hitting the bar later that night. Or tomorrow night.

Or next week, and the week after.

Which brought up a good question. Why hadn't any of

the previous women he'd done this to filed charges against him? Surely if they had, Corey wouldn't be walking around unscathed to keep doing it.

Hudson started the Jeep and drove over the curb and around the gas station. The area around the gas pumps was empty, and the traffic on the interstate was light. As they left the gas station/convenience store behind, she alternated between twisting in her seat to look out the back window and watching her side window for signs of the state police. It was hard to remain optimistic between knowing they were being hunted by the cops and Corey likely being out of jail.

"I think we're clear, why don't you eat?" Hudson suggested. "And hand me my sandwich too."

She unwrapped his ham and cheese sandwich before giving it to him. Then she unwrapped her own. Staring down at it for a moment, she decided to pray. "Dear Lord, we thank You for this food we are about to eat. We pray that You continue to watch over us and keep us safe. Also, Lord, we ask that You protect the women in Idaho from being hurt by Corey. Amen."

"Amen," Hudson echoed.

Her sandwich tasted like cardboard, but she forced herself to eat anyway. Hudson was right to concentrate on taking one step at a time.

As a trauma nurse, she knew that victims didn't always get the justice they deserved. She prayed that wouldn't be the case this time. She desperately needed to believe Corey would be held accountable for the crimes he'd committed.

And knew she'd delay going back to her old job and her life in Portland, until that happened. Doing whatever was necessary to get him behind bars.

HUDSON HAD to keep turning his head to check the oncoming traffic in the northbound lanes to make sure they hadn't drawn the attention of the state patrol. His limited vision on his left had been one reason he'd given in to let Kendra drive in the first place.

He glanced at her again, wishing there was a way to make her feel better. She'd tossed the newspaper into the back seat and was working hard to watch for cops hiding along the interstate.

Was it possible Corey hadn't gotten arrested? That the slick lawyer had somehow slipped the vial into another man's pocket?

He wouldn't put anything past the guy, that was for sure.

The longer they drove, though, the less he was concerned with getting caught. For one thing, they hadn't passed any towns. When he'd been young, there hadn't been money to spare for trips, so he wasn't familiar with this area of the state.

In fact, he knew far more about both Afghanistan and Bagdad than he did about most cities and states in the US. A somewhat depressing realization.

"There isn't much out here, is there?" He glanced at Kendra. "I didn't realize there was so much uninhabited land in Idaho."

"I think it's beautiful," she said. "But I know what you mean. This is all so very different from where I live in Portland. What about you?" She turned in her seat to watch the rear window for a few minutes before facing him. "Where do you live now that you're not in the navy any longer?"

He shrugged. "I haven't found a place yet."

"What do you mean?" She frowned. "You can't just drift from city to city."

"Why not? Jack Reacher does."

"He's not real," she shot back. "He's a character in a book series. And you have Echo to consider."

"I know, I was teasing." His teammates would be shocked to know how much he'd lightened up since meeting Kendra. "I was thinking of heading back to San Diego, that's where we were stationed."

"Oh yeah, I guess I knew that." Was it his imagination or was there a hint of disappointment in her voice?

"I've never been to Portland, what's it like?"

"Crowded, busy, but there's lots of really nice scenery there too. I guess it's not that close to the ocean, though. Not like San Diego."

He thought about the reoccurring nightmares that overwhelmed him during his migraines. The nickname for Navy SEALs was frogmen. As a guy who'd spent the better part of twenty years running ops in the ocean, it was shameful to admit he wasn't anxious to jump in again anytime soon. "I like the sound of the waves."

"Yeah, they are very soothing." She turned to stare out the back window again. "I doubt we'll see any cops this far outside of Boise."

"That could be, although they are called state police for a reason." He wasn't ready to let his guard down. "What do you suggest for a place to do another rest stop? I hate keeping Echo confined in the back for so long."

"There used to be a rest stop in Blacks Creek, but no gas station if you can believe that." She frowned and sat in her seat facing the windshield. "I'll watch for signs. I'm sure Echo would prefer to be active."

"He would." Hudd would like to let the dog run for a

bit. Normally, he'd run alongside him, but the migraine he'd suffered earlier hadn't quite gone away. There was a lingering pain along his left temple, the location of his injury. And since he wasn't always sure what brought the attacks on, he thought it better to remain low-key. His top priority was getting the journal and their story to the FBI.

Once they'd gotten the Feds involved, he needed to convince Kendra to head back to Portland. He wanted her far away from Robinson and Barkley.

"Can you check local news on your phone?"

"Yes, good idea." She pulled out her phone, then hesitated. "I still have it turned off to preserve the battery. I should have looked to see if they sold charging cords at the convenience store."

Her comment made him pull out his decrepit phone too. "I have less than ten percent battery left, and there's no signal out here." He handed it to her. "Turn it off for me, would you?"

She did, then tucked her phone back in her purse. "I'll hold off using my phone too. There probably isn't good coverage. Besides, there's nothing I can do about Corey getting out of jail. I have to put the situation in God's hands and pray Corey doesn't hurt anyone else. And we may need to use it for something more important."

"I admire your faith, Kendra." He reached over to take her hand. "You've shown me what I've been missing these past few years."

"I'm glad to help." She smiled, and his heart literally skipped in his chest. He needed to get a grip. Distractions could get a man killed. He took a moment to eyeball the rearview mirror and his side-view mirror. So far, so good. "I can't say it's been easy, though. Losing Olivia was awful."

"I can only imagine."

"You lost your teammate, which had to be just as difficult."

"Yeah. He gave the ultimate sacrifice." He continued sweeping the area for cops, glad there didn't seem to be many.

After another thirty minutes, Kendra broke the silence. "Is that a car pulled over up ahead?"

"I'm not sure." His pulse spiked at the thought of passing a cop sitting at the side of the road with a radar gun.

A strained silence shimmered between them as the Jeep ate up the miles.

"It's a pickup truck," Kendra said. "Looks pretty old and rusty. I'm sure it broke down and the owner just left it there."

He didn't say anything, scouring the area around the interstate searching for anything out of place. Using an abandoned car for cover wasn't outside the realm of possibilities.

"I don't see anyone inside," she went on. "I'm sure it's fine."

Hudd hit the gas, sending the Jeep lurching forward. He found himself holding his breath as they roared past the abandoned car. After five miles, he slowed down and released a sigh of relief.

"I guess you see danger everywhere you look," Kendra said softly.

"Occupational hazard."

They drove in silence for another few minutes. "The rest stop is still there," Kendra gestured toward the sign. "Five miles from here."

"Good. Echo will appreciate a break."

"Me too," Kendra said wryly.

He kept a wary eye out as the rest stop came into view.

The truck they'd passed had looked as if it had been there for a while, but he couldn't discount the possibility that the driver had walked there.

The diagonal parking spaces in front of the rest stop were empty except for a large eighteen-wheeler. Even as they got off on the ramp, the driver of the truck emerged from the bathrooms, hitched his jeans, and hopped into the driver's seat. Hudson pulled in and waited for the truck to leave before pushing open his driver's side door.

"I feel bad for the person whose truck broke down," Kendra said.

He was glad the traffic had been light, most of the vehicles they'd seen were large semitrucks or other types of trucks. He opened the back hatch and let Echo out. The dog raced around, then headed right out to a grassy area to do his business.

"I'm going inside for a minute," Kendra said.

"We'll wait here." He pulled a ball from the back of his Jeep and tossed it for Echo. The dog eagerly ran after it, catching it on the second bounce.

Echo would do this all day if Hudd let him, but he didn't mind letting the dog burn off some energy. He threw the ball again while watching the highway.

Echo ran like the wind, jumping so high he cleared three feet before landing back on the ground. Hudd had considered creating some sort of obstacle course for the dog, but that would mean putting down roots.

Something he hadn't really considered until now.

Portland sounded more metropolitan than he'd have liked. He gazed out at the Blacks Creek landscape, appreciating the wide open space. It was probably too far away to be practical, no grocery store, gas station, or restaurant to be found. But he wouldn't mind a place similar to where he'd grown up. His memories of Eagle weren't all bad.

Kendra was a trauma critical care nurse, and he suspected that most trauma centers were located in the heart of big cities, not out in the middle of nowhere Idaho, Montana, or Wyoming.

He shrugged off the thought. This wasn't the time to be thinking about where he might settle down.

Or if Kendra would be a part of that decision.

Echo didn't return with the ball. He was sniffing around, no doubt picking up an interesting scent. "Echo, come!" he shouted.

The dog whirled, picked up the ball, and loped toward him. He bent down to retrieve the ball, and when he straightened, he caught sight of a vehicle cresting a hill in the distance heading toward them.

Too far away to make out the model, but he glanced nervously toward the restrooms. Where was Kendra? He wanted to head around back to avoid being seen, but he couldn't leave her behind.

Hudd hurried toward the woman's restroom. "Kendra? You okay?"

"Coming," she responded. He heard water in the sink, then the sound of a hand dryer.

The vehicle was approaching fast. No sirens blaring, and he couldn't make out if it was a squad or not. Could be that the driver was ignoring the speed limit considering the lack of traffic, but the tiny hairs on the back of his neck tingled in warning.

"This way, around back." He took Kendra's arm and urged her around the back of the building. "There's a car coming up fast, could be a cop."

Kendra's gaze turned fearful. "He'll see the Jeep."

"I know." Hudd raked his gaze over the area. "We need a place to hide."

"Out here? What's the point? They'll find us eventually." She stared at him as if he were crazy.

"Hurry." He lightly jogged across the uneven terrain. They were on a hill overlooking the creek, and they could go down along the edge to get out of sight. Kendra ran to keep up with him while Echo treated this as another game.

The moment he reached the edge, he pulled Kendra down to the ground. The creek bed was down below, and the rocky landscape was somewhat precarious.

"I need you to go down as low as you can. I'll watch from here."

"What are you going to do?" Kendra asked.

He pulled his weapon. "Hold them off. See if your phone works. If you can get through to the Feds, let them know what's happening."

"Okay." She pulled out her phone and turned it on. Then she gingerly moved down the rocky hill toward the creek below.

"Guard, Echo," Hudson said to the dog.

Echo wheeled around to follow Kendra. Hudd hoped he was wrong about the vehicle that had been speeding toward the rest station, but he didn't think so.

He found a place along the ridge where he could stretch out on his stomach while still being able to see the area around the rest station. It didn't take long for the vehicle to pull in and park next to his Jeep.

It wasn't a squad but a large 4x4 RAM truck, silver in color. It looked familiar. Then it clicked. The truck had been in the driveway of Barkley's house.

A man emerged from the truck, carrying a rifle. He

stood for a moment until another older man joined him, also carrying a weapon.

The pair was father and son, but not Andrew and George Barkley as he'd expected. No, the two men were Tristan and Coach Donahue.

CHAPTER FIFTEEN

Flanked by Echo, Kendra slipped over the rocky terrain while holding up her phone to get a signal. Unfortunately, she had only one bar.

One stinking bar. She swallowed hard trying to hold back a flash of panic.

Maybe it would be enough.

"Kendra?" Hudson's low whisper had her turning to head back toward him. "Tristan and Coach Donahue are here each armed with rifles. Your phone?"

Tristan and Coach Donahue? She could hardly believe it. The pair had never seemed like viable suspects, then again, Tristan was probably the one who'd killed Zoey, and his father was just bailing him out.

Still, she was keenly disappointed the killer wasn't Corey or Andrew.

She punched in the numbers 911 and prayed the signal would go through. Her pulse quickened when she heard ringing on the other end of the line, then the sound of a dispatcher asking, "What's your emergency?"

"We're at the Blacks Creek rest area, there are two men carrying guns. Please send help!"

"Ma'am? I'm sorry, I couldn't hear what you said. Where are you?"

"Blacks Creek." She enunciated as clearly as possible while trying to be quiet enough so Tristan and his father couldn't hear. "Men with guns. Hurry!"

"Ma'am? Are you there?"

Kendra closed her eyes and hit the end button on the phone. She met Hudson's gaze and shook her head. "She can't hear me."

"Follow the creek farther from me," Hudson whispered. "Take Echo and stay safe."

"What about you?" She didn't like the idea of leaving him here. Especially not when Tristan and his father had rifles. She didn't know anything about guns, but Hudson's pistol probably didn't have the range of a rifle.

"Go," he said tersely.

"Echo, stay," she said before turning and retracing her steps to follow the edge of the creek. If she had to leave, then she'd feel better leaving Echo with Hudson. He'd need the dog more than she would.

"Go, Echo," Hudson whispered. She glanced over her shoulder, glad the dog hadn't moved. Unusual since the animal normally listened to Hudson without question.

There was a large boulder twenty yards ahead. She picked up her pace until she could drop down behind it. It was large enough to shield her from view but not too far away from Hudson's location either.

If anything happened to Hudson or Echo, she didn't think her chances of escaping through the wilderness were very good. Especially not when two men were armed with rifles.

As she huddled beside the cold rock, she realized she wasn't afraid of dying. Not when it meant she'd be taken home to God, reunited with her daughter, Olivia, her mother, Grace, and Zoey.

But she would miss Hudson. More than she thought possible. And for a long moment she longed for something she never thought she'd find.

A man to share her life with.

She drew in a deep breath and let it out slowly. They weren't beaten yet. Hudson was a former Navy SEAL. If anyone could get them out of this, he could.

Yet if that couldn't happen, then she would be okay.

You're in charge, Lord. I'm putting myself in Your loving hands. Let thy will be done. Amen.

KENDRA HADN'T GONE FAR ENOUGH, and Echo wasn't listening either. But Hudd didn't have time to worry about either of them.

His only thought was to neutralize the threat.

The Donahues must be avid hunters because they each took a post on one side of the restroom, making themselves smaller targets. He didn't dare move, knowing they would slowly rake their respective scopes over the area to look for him.

They were roughly a hundred yards away, a makeable shot for him. He wasn't the sharpshooter on the team, Dallas held that honor. But he was second best. He'd make the shot.

The problem would be that he could only take out one target at a time. And doing so would likely reveal his position. The rocky edge was too unpredictable to shoot, then run to a new location.

He'd just have to trust his aim and hope that taking them by surprise would work to his advantage.

He kept his head low and patiently waited, watching for them to make their move. He had no idea how much hunting Tristan and his father had done over the years, but he had to assume they were good enough to take him out. Having a rifle and a scope would be to their advantage.

A hint of movement caught his eye. Another man was creeping up to the building housing the restrooms, having come out from behind Hudd's Jeep. His gut clenched as he worried it would be another shooter he'd be forced to contend with.

Yet the stealthy nature of the guy seemed to indicate otherwise. It wasn't long until Hudson recognized Nevins.

Friend or foe? He couldn't be sure.

The glimpse of sunlight reflected off the scope of the rifle on the farthest side of the building. Hudson ducked his head as a shot rang out.

Thankfully, it missed, but Hudson didn't waste a second. He eased back up and fired at the spot where the shooter was standing. A loud cry indicated he'd hit his target.

One down, two to go.

"Drop your weapons and put your hands where I can see them!" The voice sounded like Nevins, but Hudson didn't move from his location.

"Hey, he shot at us!" a whiney voice protested.

"Now!" Nevins barked.

Hudson frowned, wondering if this was a ploy to get him to reveal himself. He remained still, listening intently. There was a thudding noise as something heavy hit the dirt.

"I'm hurt," another voice said. "He shot me!"

"You shot first," Nevins said. "Throw down your weapon."

There were muffled sounds as if Coach had complied too. But Hudson still didn't move. From his vantage point, he could see Kendra poking her head up, looking at him curiously. He scowled and shook his head.

"Hudson, I have Tristan and Eric Donahue in custody," Nevins called. "It's safe to come out."

Hudd didn't move for a long moment. Then he risked a quick glance over the edge of the bluff. Both Donahue men were handcuffed, their rifles tossed on the ground. Nevins seemed to catch his eye, and for a long moment, Hudd expected the worst.

"I know you don't trust me, Foster. But I am one of the good guys," Nevins called.

Hudd knew he could take out Nevins from here if necessary. One target was easier than two. But he hesitated, unwilling to blithely shoot a cop.

"Why were the police staked out at the Boise FBI office?" Hudson asked in a voice loud enough to carry across the terrain. "You're the only one who knew that was where we were headed."

"I know, that was my fault. I felt obligated to report up through the chain of command about Zoey's journal. Next thing I know, Barkley knew all about it and sent several guys there." There was a brief pause before Nevins said, "I knew you wouldn't be caught by the cops waiting at the FBI office, and Salt Lake was closer than Portland, so I decided to stake out this section of the highway. I was hiding in the abandoned truck, making sure my vehicle was out of sight. After I saw you go past, I waited until the Donahues showed up, then followed them here."

Hudson wasn't convinced. He glanced one more time at Kendra who was watching him warily, then asked, "Why did you suspect Tristan and his dad? You weren't at the party that night."

"That's true, but after you left me searching for the handcuff key, I remembered that all the guys were hungover the next day. All except for Tristan. And it made me think, what if that was because Tristan wasn't drinking with the rest of them? What if he was out with Zoey, killing her, and then stashing the body?"

It was plausible, Hudd had to give him that.

"I'm not the bad guy," Nevins repeated in a frustrated tone.

"Prove it by holstering your gun," Hudson said.

To his surprise, Nevins did. He holstered his weapon and pushed the two men up against the wall of the restrooms. Then he stood with his hands facing palm outward. "I'm not here to arrest you, Foster."

Hudd quickly scrambled up over the rim of the ledge. Nevins didn't move, simply watching as he approached.

"FYI, Tristan here smokes." Nevins nodded toward the younger Donahue. "If you still have that cigarette butt, we can try to lift his prints."

"I do. And I have a smashed bullet fragment that I dug out of the cave wall." Hudd eyed Nevins warily. "Did you call for backup?"

"Yeah, but understand they're not going to be here for a few minutes yet." Nevins glanced over his shoulder. "Where's Kendra?"

"She's safe."

"Hudd, you need to put your weapon away. The guys coming to back me up will not look kindly on you holding a gun on me."

That was true. He turned to look at Coach Donahue and his son. The older man looked pale, blood seeping from a wound in his shoulder. Tristan looked panicked. Neither man had spoken since being handcuffed. Hudd decided to bluff them a bit. "We have Zoey's journal and the cigarette butt Tristan left behind at the scene of the shooting, along with the slug that I'm sure will be matched to one of those rifles. Oh, and the make and model of the car that you used to try to run us down." He managed a smile. "You're both going down for first degree murder."

"I didn't mean to kill her," Tristan blurted. "It was an accident! We were arguing and I—lost my temper. I didn't mean to do it!"

Hudd glanced back at Nevins who was listening to this confession with interest. "And what about Jeanie Mayberry?" the cop asked.

Tristan shot a quick glance at his father but didn't say anything. The former coach hung his head. "We were trying to frame you, Foster. You should have been arrested for Zoey's murder twenty years ago. I still don't understand why George let you go."

Nevins snorted. "You need evidence to press charges, Donahue. Which we now have against the both of you. And I was here watching as you fired at Foster first, Coach. So his claim of self-defense will stand."

"I'll testify too," Kendra said breathlessly. Hudd had been so focused on whether or not he could trust Nevins that he hadn't heard her approach. "You're both going to jail for a long time."

The father and son team glanced at each other but didn't say anything. Until Tristan finally muttered, "My dad needs medical care."

"Yeah, we'll get right on that," Nevins said dryly.

Hudd finally slid his Sig Sauer back into its holster. Thankfully, Nevins didn't immediately reach for his weapon. Instead, the cop took a step forward and held out his hand. "It's an honor to meet you, Hudson. I'm sorry for messing things up."

"I would apologize for not trusting you, but I'd probably do it again under the same set of circumstances." Hudd took his hand. "Thanks for not shooting me."

"Likewise," Nevins said with a nod.

"Does this mean the danger is over?" Kendra took a step closer, eyeing both of the Donahue men.

Hudd couldn't help himself. He reached out and gently pulled her into his arms. He cradled her close, the way he'd wanted to from the first moment they'd met, when she still believed he'd killed Zoey. "Yes, it's over. You're safe now, Kendra."

"And you too, Hudson," she whispered. Then she wrapped her arms around his neck and drew him down for a long kiss.

He clutched her to him, wishing the kiss never had to end. But all too soon he heard the wail of police sirens. Kendra broke off their kiss but continued holding him. "I'm so glad you're okay," she said. "When you went over to talk to David, I feared he'd kill you."

"Gee, thanks," Nevins said dryly.

"I'm sorry, but you have to admit sending cops to the FBI office was enough to make us suspicious of your intent," Kendra said in a scolding voice. "You should have trusted us to get to the FBI on our own."

"I know. But following orders is something that is deeply ingrained by the military." Nevins glanced at him. "Except maybe for Navy SEALs."

"We follow orders too," Hudd protested. "But we're

probably given more leeway during our ops than your average soldier."

"No doubt," Nevins agreed.

Two squads pulled into the rest area. Hudson quickly pressed the two dog baggies, one with the cigarette butt and the other with the smashed bullet into Nevins's hand. "The evidence," he said in a low voice.

"Thanks."

He tensed when he recognized Andrew Barkley getting out of one squad while another guy he didn't recognize slid out from the other.

"What's going on here?" Barkley demanded.

The guy might not be a murderer, but he had groped his own sister, and that was enough for Hudd to dislike him more than he had already. "We found your sister's journal and her killer." He gestured toward the Donahue men. "Interesting that you weren't able to solve the crime over all these years, isn't it? Is that because you knew what Zoey had written in her journal? That you were afraid of the truth coming to light?"

Barkley's face reddened with anger, but he managed to keep it in check. "I don't know what you're talking about."

"You will," Hudd said, offering an insincere smile. "Zoey's journal is a wealth of interesting information. Especially about you."

"How do you know it's hers?" Barkley demanded.

"Oh, I'm sure the handwriting experts will be able to verify the journal is hers. Plus Kendra remembered Zoey writing in it and found it at the tree where they used to sit down by the creek." Hudd pinned him with a steely glare. "Kendra's a well-respected trauma critical care nurse. I'm sure her testimony will carry a lot of weight. The journal will be used as evidence of criminal activity."

All color leeched from Barkley's face.

"Let's get back to how these two men tried to kill us," Kendra said. "No thanks to you, Andrew."

"I'm a witness, Chief, and I have evidence too," Nevins added. "Not only that, but Tristan here confessed to killing Zoey while implicating his old man in Jeanie's murder. They were trying to set Foster up for both crimes."

"Both Hudson and I heard their confessions," Kendra added. "That makes three credible witnesses, including your own military veteran officer."

Barkley scowled. "Who shot Eric Donahue?"

"I did, after he shot at me, first," Hudd said. "I had better aim."

"He's telling the truth, I saw the whole thing," Nevins said. "Hudson is a former Navy SEAL. If he'd wanted Donahue dead, trust me, he'd be dead."

Barkley clearly realized there was nothing he could do but to go along with Nevins's statement. But he avoided Hudd's gaze. "Campbell, get these suspects into the squad and take them back to Eagle. We'll file charges and let the DA know what went down here."

Campbell hastened to follow Chief Barkley's orders. There was a long moment before Barkley turned away. "I'll expect your report on my desk ASAP, Nevins," he said.

"Yes, sir."

Hudd let out a long breath. "I'll give you Zoey's journal, but I need you to promise me something."

"What's that?" Nevins asked warily.

"That you run for chief of police once Barkley steps down." Hudd grinned. "After the contents of Zoey's journal hits the newspapers, there's no way he'll be able to keep his job."

Nevins smiled. "Done."

"Do you know if Corey Robinson is still in jail?" Kendra asked.

"He is, yes. The judge denied him bail." Nevins shrugged. "It was another reason I thought of Tristan. Turns out, Robinson was in court all day, then at his office with a client until very late during the time frame of Jeanie's murder. He's a rapist, but he had an alibi for Jeanie's murder."

"Well, I'm glad he's still in jail." Kendra looked relieved. "I would like to testify against him."

"Me too," Hudd added.

"I'll make a note of that," Nevins said. "Are you guys heading back to Eagle?"

Hudd glanced at Kendra. "That's up to you."

She looked surprised, then nodded. "I need to talk to my dad, let him know what happened here."

They walked back to where Hudson had left his Jeep. He took out Zoey's journal and handed it to Nevins. "I'll give you a lift to your car."

Nevins had left his squad behind an outcropping of rock on the opposite side of the highway a few yards from the rusty abandoned truck. Nevins used his radio to let the dispatcher know he was returning to town, then glanced at him again. "If you decide you want a job as a cop, let me know. We could use someone like you, Hudson."

Hudd touched the corner of his left eye. "I don't think I'd pass the physical, but thanks."

"I'd still hire you," Nevins insisted. "You're accurate with a gun, despite your left eye. Clearly, your skills far surpass most of the guys I work with." Then Nevins flushed. "Well, I guess I should wait to see if I even have a shot at being in charge before I start offering jobs."

Hudd shook hands with the cop again, then watched as

he left. Kendra came out of the passenger seat to stand beside him. Echo whined from the back of the Jeep, so Hudd let him out for a quick run.

"I'm glad he's one of the good guys," Kendra said.

"Me too. My gut wanted to trust him, but I wasn't willing to risk your life on sheer instinct." He waited for Echo to finish watering a half dozen bushes, then Hudson turned to face her. "I'd like to visit you in Portland, maybe find a place to live there."

"You would?" She looked surprised, then her gaze turned thoughtful. "I'm not sure I see you settling in a busy city."

"Kendra, I'll be happy as long as you're there." He caught her hand and tugged her close. "I've fallen in love with you. I had a goofy crush on you back in high school, but I know things wouldn't have worked out back then. Even though I was injured on our last op, I wouldn't trade my time with the SEALs for anything. Those experiences, good and bad, have made me into the man I am today. I think—God brought us together here in Idaho for a reason."

"Oh, Hudson." Her eyes were bright with tears. "I've fallen in love with you too. And I know God brought us together now because we can finally appreciate each other the way we never would have been able to twenty years ago."

"Exactly." He bent his head and kissed her. Echo nudged them with his nose as if wanting to be included in the embrace.

They clung together for several long moments. Then he heard a chopper overhead. He broke off from the kiss, frowning as he looked up at the low-flying bird.

"Get under the Jeep," he ordered, desperate for Kendra

to be shielded from the threat. But then he saw a familiar face plastered up against the window and a hand waving.

Was that Kaleb? He stared, then recognized the pilot was Dawson Steele. What in the world were these guys doing here?

"Hold on, Kendra." He stood waiting with Echo on his blind side. The whirlybird landed on a flat portion of the terrain about a hundred yards away.

The blades slowly stopped spinning, and Dawson and Kaleb jumped out from the chopper. Hudd was surprised to see them both and brought Kendra along to meet them. "You old dawg, how did you know where to find me?"

"Watch who you're calling old." Dawson smacked him on the back while Kaleb gave him a one-armed hug. "I'm a year younger than you, hombre."

"Nico's the baby," Kaleb pointed out. "And we found you by calling in a whole lot of favors within law enforcement. Figured you might need a ride."

Hudd shook his head in amazement. "Who owns the bird?"

"A neighbor," Dawson answered somewhat evasively. The guy looked thinner than Hudd remembered and hoped his abdominal surgery after taking shrapnel in the gut wasn't the reason. "I'm a certified chopper pilot."

"We came ASAP because I was worried about you." Kaleb eyed Kendra curiously. "Ma'am, I'm Kaleb Tyson and this is Dawg a.k.a. Dawson Steele. We're a couple of Hudd's SEAL teammates."

"This is Kendra Pickett," Hudd quickly introduced her. "And I'm sure you both remember Echo. Sorry, I guess I'm still dazed by Dawson and Kaleb showing up in a freaking helicopter. And where are your dogs?"

"Dillon, Montana, isn't that far," Dawson pointed out.

"I left Kilo with my dad and met up with Kaleb up in Boise."

"Charlotte is with Sierra," Kaleb added. "I found a flight right after your phone call, Hudd. Glad I did."

Hudd was touched that the guys had gone all out for him. But it wasn't necessary. "I'm fine and so is Kendra. It was a little dicey an hour or so ago, but we're good now."

"Glad to hear it. But you could have called us in earlier," Kaleb said with a hint of exasperation in his tone. "We would have been here to cover your six."

"For sure," Dawson agreed. "Next time, you need to let us in on the fun."

Hudd's grin faded. "Hopefully there won't be a next time."

"Nico has a lead on Simon Normandy's a.k.a. Simon Marks's whereabouts. The guy was last seen in Irvine, California. He's going to let us know if he needs us to back him up."

At Kendra's confused look, Hudd explained. "Nico is another member of the team. He's been searching for Jaydon's younger sister, Ava, who has been missing for what, almost two months now?"

Kaleb and Dawson nodded.

"And Jaydon is the teammate who didn't make it home?" Kendra asked.

"Yes, ma'am." Dawson hooked his thumbs on his jeans, which hung a little on his much leaner frame, thanks to his recent weight loss. It wouldn't have surprised Hudd if the former frogman had taken to wearing a cowboy hat to go with his cowboy boots. "Jaydon would expect us to find Ava, and Nico is determined to do just that."

"Well then, it sounds to me like all of you should go join

Nico in Irvine," Kendra said. "That girl needs your help. And who better to find her than a group of Navy SEALs?"

Hudd wanted to hug and kiss her for that, but he managed to restrain himself to simply taking her hand. "Trust me, we will the moment Nico gives us the word. Right now, he's still fishing for intel."

"So what happened here?" Kaleb asked, his gaze bouncing curiously between Kendra and Hudd. "What kind of trouble have you been getting into?"

"We managed to solve a twenty-year-old murder," Hudd said. "Thanks to Kendra's persistence."

"You kept us safe long enough to find what we needed." Her smile faded, a serious expression darkening her amber eyes. "And thanks to Hudson, we took a sexual predator off the streets."

"Wow, you've been busy," Dawson said with admiration.

"We have." Kendra turned to face him. "I love you, Hudson Foster."

"And I love you too." He didn't care that both his teammates gaped in shock at this proclamation. "Guys, looks like I'll be relocating to Portland, Oregon."

"No, I was thinking I'd look for a new job at a hospital in San Diego," Kendra argued. "The more I think about it, the more I like the idea of living closer to the ocean."

"Well, it looks to me like Hudd's got his hair in the butter," Dawson drawled.

"What?" Kendra asked in confusion.

"He means I'm in a sticky situation, but he's wrong," Hudd explained. "Don't listen to his goofy cowboy phrases. The Dawg swims better than he rides a horse."

"Not true," Dawson drawled. "I excel at both activities."

Kaleb rolled his eyes. "Whatever. Do you guys want a ride back to civilization or not?"

"Not," Hudd and Kendra said at the same time. Then they both laughed.

"Now that's great to hear," Dawson said. He clapped Hudd on the back. "You need to laugh more often, bro. Come on, Kaleb. I'll need to get the bird back to its owner. Sylvie will rip me a new one if I don't."

"Who is Sylvie?" Kaleb asked as they turned away.

"My neighbor," he said on a sigh. "And a royal pain in the back end of a horse."

Kendra giggled, and Hudd hugged her again. Once the chopper lifted off, carrying Dawson and Kaleb away, he asked, "You'd really move to San Diego?"

"I'd move anywhere for you, Hudson. Because love is all that matters."

"Ditto, Kendra." He kissed her again, silently thanking God for bringing Kendra back into his life when he needed her the most.

EPILOGUE

The following week passed in a flurry of activity. Over the course of several days, Kendra provided lengthy statements covering the sequence of events starting with her returning to town. She was kept in a small room separate from Hudson, which seemed silly because they'd been together nonstop over the past tension-filled days. She spent hours with Officer Campbell going through every minute detail, including Corey Robinson's attempt to drug her.

Hudson had been treated the same way, only he was interrogated by David Nevins. As expected, the contents of Zoey's journal were leaked to the press, resulting in Andrew Barkley's resignation as police chief. His second in command, Bryce Townsend, was put in charge, but the guy didn't have near the amount of experience that David did. David had been a military police officer in the army as well as working here in town over the past ten years.

She really hoped David was given the job of police chief. He deserved it more than any of Andrew's cronies did.

Kendra's father had been stunned to learn of the danger

surrounding her and Hudson. He'd been hurt about being lied to, but she'd hugged him close and promised to never do something like that again, reassuring him that she loved him and had only lied to keep him safe.

Today she and Hudson had an afternoon meeting with the DA's office related to the confession of Tristan and his father. When they were finished, the ADA informed them he wouldn't need anything else unless the Donahues decided to take the case to trial. Which didn't seem likely since Tristan confessed and a search warrant of the coach's black SUV revealed evidence of Jeanie's DNA from where he'd stuck her body in the back to get her out to the cave.

At this point, both the Donahue men were looking to cut the best deal possible.

"What about Corey Robinson?" Kendra drilled the ADA with a narrow gaze. "I want to press charges against him for drugging my drink."

"I know you do, but the Boise PD has already charged him with three counts of date rape, thanks to the women who came forward after hearing of his initial arrest. Trust me, he won't see the light of day for a very long time."

"That doesn't stop Kendra from pressing charges too, does it?" Hudson asked.

"No, but . . ." The ADA grimaced and shrugged.

"It's okay." She put a reassuring hand on Hudson's arm. "Sounds like these other women have more to testify to than I do."

"Are you sure?" His concern warmed her heart. He'd been a rock through all of this, which was more time-consuming and emotionally draining than she ever could have imagined.

"Yes. I'm sure." She knew it was time to let it go. Corey

would get what he deserved. She shouldn't waste any more time thinking about him.

But she did pray for his victims, those who had already come forward and those who hadn't. Because she knew there were probably several still out there wondering what had happened.

It was close to dinnertime when they left the DA's office. "I told your dad I'd pick up Chinese for dinner," Hudson said. "If that's okay with you?"

"My favorite." She wasn't surprised at how well her father and Hudson were getting along. Her dad admired Hudson for serving his country and for keeping her safe over those harrowing days when Tristan and his father were trying to silence her.

"I called in an order, shouldn't take long to grab it." Hudson was still driving his blue Jeep with Echo in the back. She'd grown to love the dog as much as Hudson did.

They hadn't really discussed next steps. Hudson seemed content to hang out for a while in Eagle, and she couldn't go back to work yet anyway. Her shoulder was feeling better, so she'd decided to hold off on seeing the surgeon until her regular checkup scheduled for the following week.

When Hudson returned with the food, the enticing scent of sweet and sour pork, sesame chicken, and soy sauce filled the interior of the Jeep. Echo had his nose pressed to the crate as if some of the food was earmarked for him.

At the house, Hudson carried the bag of Chinese inside. Then he surprised her by handing her a small fortune cookie. "Will you open this for me?"

"Dessert before dinner?" she teased. She glanced at her father who was watching her rather than opening the white containers. Echo hovered close to her side. When she broke the cookie open, a diamond ring dropped into the palm of her hand. She blinked in surprise. "What's this?"

Hudson dropped to one knee, and Echo comically stretched out beside him. "Kendra, will you please marry me? I asked your father for permission, and he agreed as long as I promise to bring you back home often to visit."

"Yes, Hudson." Her eyes filled with tears, but these came from joy, not sorrow. She vowed not to cry over what had happened in the past but to continue moving forward. She couldn't help but smile at the way Echo's tail wagged back and forth as if he sensed the excitement in the air. "I'd be honored to marry you."

"I love you." Hudson took a moment to slide the ring onto her finger, then stood and swept her into his arms.

"I love you too." She kissed Hudson and then grinned at her father, who was wiping tears from his eyes.

This time, she knew she was marrying the man God had chosen for her. And she couldn't wait to see what their lives together would bring.

From this moment on.

I HOPE you enjoyed Hudson and Kendra's story in *Sealed with Justice*. Are you ready for Dawson and Sylvie's story in *Sealed with Strength*? Click here!

DEAR READER

I hope you are enjoying my Called to Protect series. I'm having fun writing about these Navy SEAL heroes who are struggling with the pain of losing a teammate while trying to adapt to civilian life. The least I could do was help them find love. I hope you enjoyed Hudson and Kendra's journey to their happily ever after.

I'm hard at work finishing up Dawson and Sylvie's story in *Sealed with Strength*. My goal is to have all six books finished before the end of the year, although I do have several books under contract with Harlequin too. Trust me, I'm writing as fast as I can!

I adore hearing from my readers! I can be found through my website at https://www.laurascottbooks.com, via Facebook at https://www.facebook.com/LauraScott Books, Instagram at https://www.instagram.com/laurascott books/, and Twitter https://twitter.com/laurascottbooks. Also, take a moment to sign up for my monthly newsletter, all subscribers receive a free novella, *Starting Over*, that is not available for purchase on any platform.

Until next time,

Laura Scott

PS: If you're interested in a sneak peek of *Sealed with Strength*, I've included the first chapter here.

SEALED WITH STRENGTH

Chapter One

Sylvie McLane tugged her cowboy hat down on her head as she led her favorite mare, Fanny, along the north ridge of the McLane Mountain Ranch. After her father's cancer diagnosis, she'd taken over running the ranch, which had grown over the thirty-eight years her father had owned it. McLane Mountain was one of the most prosperous ranches in the area, and she was proud of what she and her dad had accomplished.

Her job now was to keep it going. No small feat in lean times of falling beef prices combined with the fact that most of the cowboys working for her chafed at taking orders from a woman. As if she hadn't learned anything in the past thirty-five years she'd lived and worked here.

She preferred raising and training horses, but she wouldn't allow that to hold her back from taking over all aspects of the ranch. It was clear her younger brother Sean wasn't going to be much help.

"Whoa, girl," she murmured, tugging slightly on

Fanny's reins to halt their progress. This spot offered the best view of the entire ranch, all fifteen hundred acres of it. The impressive sight never ceased to amaze her.

The gunshot came out of nowhere. Fanny shied, rising on her hind legs and pawing the air with her front hooves. Sylvie clenched her knees to stay seated, but Fanny turned so abruptly she felt herself losing her grip. Then Fanny rose again, throwing Sylvie off before bolting into the woods.

She hit the ground hard and rolled toward the edge of the ridge. Digging her hands into the earth, she tried to halt her momentum, but gravity pulled her toward the drop off. She managed to find a tree root and clung to it with all the strength she possessed.

It was enough to stop her free fall. Yet her lower legs dangled over the edge. Using her toes, she tried to push against the cliff wall to lever herself up. It didn't work. If anything, she slipped another two inches lower. Now more of her body was over the edge than not. The muscles in her arms quivered with exertion.

No! She couldn't die here today!

Sylvie swallowed hard and tried again to pull herself up. She was accustomed to physical labor but couldn't seem to get a good enough grip on the root. The flash of panic was impossible to ignore. How much longer could she hang here like a trout dangling from a line?

Not long.

A male hand clamped around one wrist, then the other. "I've got you."

Dawson Steele's face loomed over her, his features partially shadowed by the wide brim of his black cowboy hat. His blue eyes were full of concern as he held her. Normally, she'd be upset by his trespassing on her land. But when he began pulling her upright, she was keenly grateful for his strength.

Inch by inch, he pulled her up over the edge of the ridge. When she was mostly on solid ground, she was able to help by using her knees to scramble the rest of the way. Finally, Dawson let her go and rolled over onto his back, his hands pressing against his abdomen. A large tan dog that looked like a yellow lab came over to sniff at him, then licked his face.

"Thank you." She frowned when Dawson seemed to be battling pain. "Hey, are you all right?"

"Yeah." The strain in his voice indicated otherwise. "Just need a minute."

She tried not to read too much into his comment, yet she knew she was sturdy and weighed a hundred and twenty-five pounds. No lightweight, that was for sure. Dawson had obviously hurt himself pulling her to safety.

Finally, he pushed himself into a sitting position. He looped his arm around his dog, then glanced at her. "I had several abdominal surgeries over the past few months. The muscles are still tender, especially when I go overboard using them."

Abdominal surgeries, plural? "I'm sorry, I didn't know."

"How could you?" Dawson's tone held an edge. He stood and held out his hand to her. She accepted his help, trying to ignore the weird attraction she felt toward him. After twenty years of not seeing the guy while he served their country as a Navy SEAL, the past six months he'd popped in and out of her life several times.

It really annoyed her.

"Good thing that shooter didn't make his jack," Dawson drawled. She wanted to roll his eyes at his old western phrase of indicating the shooter had missed his mark. His tone was light, but his gaze was serious. "Any idea who set you in their sights?"

"I hope it wasn't you," she said tartly. "Why are you here anyway?"

He shook his head. "Still as prickly as ever, Sylvie. Why would I shoot you, then rush over to save your life? I was on Copper Creek property when I heard the gunfire. Saw you get busted off your horse, so I rode Diamond to get here as soon as I could. Thankfully, Kilo was able to keep up."

She glanced from his dog, Kilo, to Diamond, the gelding standing near a tree a few yards away. She flushed and nodded. It had been a long time since she'd been busted off a horse, that was for sure. "You're right, you did save my life. If you hadn't grabbed my arms . . ." She didn't finish the thought.

A shiver rippled down her spine as realization dawned slowly. Someone had just tried to kill her.

"I believe the gunfire came from the west," Dawson said. "Let's hop on Diamond and search for your horse."

"I might weigh too much for Diamond to carry us both," she protested.

"Don't be ridiculous. You're fine." Dawson swung himself up into the saddle, a slight grimace creasing his features. Then he held out his hand.

She accepted his grip, then stepped up on his boot to swing herself up behind him. The saddle made riding together uncomfortable. She did her best to ignore being plastered up against Dawson. Hopefully, Fanny hadn't gone too far. The mare was known to be sure-footed, which is why she'd chosen her to ride the mountainside.

The gunfire had been close. Way too close. June wasn't hunting season, so it had to have been deliberate.

Who had taken the shot?

The why was obvious. Someone wanted to take the McLane Mountain Ranch now that her father was officially retired from ranching. Sylvie didn't want to believe her brother Sean had done this. Or her father's long-time ranch foreman, Josh O'Leary.

She wouldn't put it past her ex-husband, Paul Griffin, to try something like this. But she'd heard he'd moved to Boulder, Colorado.

"Sylvie? Is that your horse?" Dawson gestured to the north.

She peered over Dawson's broad shoulder. "Yes, that's Fanny."

"Good-looking mare," he drawled.

"She's the best mountain trail horse I have." Normally, Fanny didn't startle easily, much less toss her rider. "The gunshot was too close and intended to spook her."

"Yeah, it was." He turned Diamond toward Fanny. The horses nickered a greeting to each other, making Sylvie smile despite her near-fatal fall from the cliff. "Any idea who would want you to eat dirt?"

"Unfortunately, there are several possibilities." She slid off Diamond's back. "Thanks again, Dawson."

"I'll escort you back to the ranch house."

She bent down to pat Kilo, then went over to grab Fanny's reins. She took a moment to physically examine the mare, making sure the animal wasn't hurt in any way. There were no obvious signs of injury, so she vaulted into the saddle and turned the mare toward Dawson. "I'm not going back, I need to ride the property. Thanks again."

"Hold on, Sylvie," Dawson protested. "You can't just pretend someone didn't take a shot at you."

"I'm not going to let that person prevent me from doing what's necessary." She was irritated with Dawson, partially because deep down she wanted nothing more than to head back to the ranch as he'd suggested. Every muscle in her body ached from the fall, and the idea of a long hot bath tempted her beyond reason.

"Why not use your chopper to patrol the property?" Dawson asked. "You can't make the entire fifteen hundred acres on horseback in a day."

"I'm well aware of that, but the chopper needs a new fuel gauge. Besides, my plan today was to ride the north ridge, not the entire property line."

Dawson let out an audible sigh. "Okay, lead the way."

"You don't have to come with me."

"I'm well aware of what I don't need to do," he said, parroting her words. "But this is serious, Sylvie. You could have died today."

"I know. I'll call the Beaverhead County Sheriff's office when I get back." She urged Fanny toward the trail.

"You must have some idea of who would do something like this," Dawson pressed as he fell behind her. The trail wasn't wide enough for them to ride side by side.

"Funny you mention that, Dawson, because your ranch stands to benefit if something happens to me. Sean has made it clear he'd love nothing more than to sell McLane Mountain to your father, or the next highest bidder. He wants to take the money and run."

"My old man can't afford to buy you out," Dawson said firmly. "I know our respective fathers have given each other the right of first refusal to buy the other's ranch when the time comes, but that doesn't mean zip if you don't have cash to cover the purchase. The Copper Creek Ranch is half the size of yours. If anyone would be the target, it would be you coming after me."

"I'd never do something like that." She glanced at him

over her shoulder. He looked good, too good. He was leaner than she remembered, but his recent surgeries likely played a role in that. Yet he still had the looks and the swagger she remembered. His dark hair was mostly covered by his cowboy hat, but his features were tan and rugged.

That stupid agreement their fathers had agreed to thirty-eight years ago provided the motive for Dawson to shoot at her.

Instead, he'd saved her life.

Even more irksome than knowing someone else wanted her dead was the knowledge that she owed Dawson for what he'd done.

And Sylvie McLane always paid her debts.

———

THE WOMAN WAS DRIVING him insane. Dawson had planned a nice leisurely ride until the gunfire had rung out, far closer than he'd liked. Diamond had reared at the sound, too, but he'd managed to remain seated, despite the pull on his abdominal muscles. But then Sylvie had hit the ground, rolling toward the edge of the mountain.

Was it too much to ask that she head back to the ranch to be safe?

He'd interacted with several tough women in the military, each of them could certainly hold their own in a male-dominated environment. Sylvie could too, but ironically, the military was more progressive than the Wild West. Sylvie carried a large chip on her shoulder, likely related to the macho cowboys who felt as if a woman's place was in the kitchen, barefoot and pregnant.

He tried not to imagine Sylvie in his kitchen, perhaps

barefoot and round with child. She'd punch him in the nose for even thinking about it.

Their fathers had been close, but he and Sylvie hadn't seen that much of each other. She'd been homeschooled. There were ranch gatherings where they'd run into each other, but they'd also kept busy with ranch chores. Truth be told, his main focus had been to graduate and join the military.

His dad has been disappointed but remained proud of what Dawson had accomplished. Not everyone made it through the rigorous training to become a Navy SEAL. And now that Dawson was back home, his father made it clear he wanted to hand the ranch over to him.

A gift he wasn't sure he wanted.

"There's a creek up ahead, we can stop there to water the horses," Sylvie said.

"Okay." There was no doubt in his mind she knew the mountain terrain better than he did. The hour was pushing noon, and his stomach rumbled with hunger.

The three surgeries to remove shrapnel had done a number on his overall strength and agility. Four months since the last surgery and he still didn't feel anywhere near 100 percent.

His SEAL team had run their last mission back in December. They'd successfully taken out their terrorist target, but the extraction had been a cluster. The underwater bomb had killed their teammate, Jaydon Rampart.

The rest of the team had all sustained injuries of some sort, but they'd survived. Their senior chief, Mason Gray, had lost his hearing in one ear and suffered partial hearing loss in the other. Kaleb had completely blown out his knee. Hudd had lost vision in one eye and suffered a head injury that still plagued him. Dallas had taken shrapnel to his shoulder, while Nico had suffered a rupture of his Achilles tendon. In comparison, Dawson's abdominal injuries weren't that bad.

Yet he hated feeling weak and helpless. Pulling Sylvie up where she'd dangled off the edge of the mountain had sent ripples of pain through his damaged muscles. Well worth it to save a life.

"You said there were too many to count." He pulled Diamond up beside her mare and slid out of the saddle. He bent to rub Kilo's fur, feeling bad for dragging the lab further than intended.

He'd been about to turn back to the house when the gunshot had gone off.

"Your dad, your foreman, Max Wolfe, my foreman, Josh O'Leary, my brother, oh, and possibly my ex-husband." She led Fanny by the reins toward the creek. "Is that enough for you?"

"My dad isn't part of this, Sylvie." It ticked him off that she'd even considered his old man a threat. "He wants me to take over the Copper Creek Ranch. No way does he want the responsibility of yours too."

"Okay, fine. One less possible threat, then." She sighed, then added, "I'm sorry. I'm being grumpy over something that isn't your fault."

"At least you got that right," he muttered. He swept off his hat and wiped the sweat from his brow. "I'd feel better if you headed back to the homestead. This guy could be watching us through a rifle scope right now."

"I know, Dawson. But he could do that tomorrow or the next day too." She led Fanny away after the horse had finished drinking from the stream. He did the same with Diamond while Kilo drank some water, then stretched out on the grass, content to rest. "What am I supposed to do? Hire a bodyguard?"

It was on the tip of his tongue to offer to take on that role, then he remembered he needed to help run his father's ranch. Not that Max Wolfe, their foreman, wasn't perfectly capable of doing the majority of the work. Max had done all that and more while he'd been in the navy. Yet Sylvie's comment had him wondering about the guy.

Why would the foreman of the Copper Creek Ranch want to harm Sylvie? The only way that made sense was if Wolfe thought he would be next in line to take over his father's ranch, if Dawson decided to leave.

Had Wolfe learned of his conversations with his father?

"I can help protect you as often as possible," he said. "I know we're both busy helping our fathers, but I don't want anything to happen to you."

She glanced at him in surprise. "I didn't realize you were taking over for your dad."

"I'm helping him out, temporarily." He wished he didn't have the ranch hanging like a yoke around his neck. "He fell and broke his hip. He's actually recovering fairly well, but he can't ride yet."

"How devastating," Sylvie said with a frown. "I can understand, though, my dad is in a similar boat. I love riding; it's the best part of owning a ranch."

"Me too." Riding horseback was something he enjoyed, although he'd liked being in the water too. Which was why he wasn't thrilled about possibly sticking around in Montana, miles from the ocean. "We need to head back. I can't help feeling vulnerable out here without any indication of where the threat is coming from."

"Fine, we can head back, but I'd like to take a less-traveled path to avoid being seen." She eyed him thoughtfully.

"Are you hungry? I have two sandwiches and am happy to share."

"Ah, sure." He was touched by her offer. For once, Sylvie was attempting to be nice. "Thanks."

They sat on the ground across from each other. Kilo came over to curl up next to his side. Dawson stroked the dog as he ate.

"It's been an uphill battle since my dad's cancer diagnosis," Sylvie said. "I've taken over all the work, but the guys treat me like I'm some sort of impostor who knows nothing about ranching."

"Because they're cowboys." He waved his hand. "They're not really dissing you, Sylvie, it's just that they're used to taking orders from your father or Josh." He paused, then asked, "Why did you list your ex-husband as a possible suspect?"

Her cheeks went pink, and she didn't answer for a long moment. "More out of revenge than anything. The marriage wasn't working, he didn't like it that I was so involved in running the ranch."

"So what, he thought he should run it?"

"No, I think he figured my dad would run it while we just sat around and took in the profits." She scowled. "I soon realized I was happier outside doing ranch chores than being with him, so I told him to take a hike. He wasn't happy with me."

Ouch. Dawson could understand why. "What's his name?"

"Paul Griffin. Although I think he moved to Boulder, Colorado, so it may be a stretch to consider him a suspect."

"Shouldn't be too difficult to find out if that's really where he's living now."

"Maybe the gunfire was a poacher," Sylvie said. "I

mean, everyone out here knows how to shoot a gun, both handgun and rifle. I'm not that small of a target, and if the shooter was using a scope, they shouldn't have missed."

"His goal may have been to make it look like an accident," Dawson pointed out.

"Maybe." She balled up the paper sandwich wrapping and took his too, stashing them into the saddle bag. "We'll go down lizard trail, it's the long way to get back but should help keep us hidden from view."

"Whatever you think is best." He wasn't about to argue. This was her ranch, her land. Just looking at Sylvie with her dark hair pulled back from her face, he knew ranching was in her blood.

It made him mad that someone wanted to take it from her.

He glanced at Kilo, debating whether or not to carry the dog in his arms down the lizard trail. "How steep is it? Will Kilo be okay?"

She hesitated, then nodded. "I think so. The horses will take it slow and easy. He looks like he'll be able to keep up."

"Okay, we'll see how it goes. If he struggles, then I'll carry him."

"Does Kilo like being carried while on the back of a horse?"

"Not particularly, but he'll do what I ask of him. That's the kind of dog he is." His training of Kilo had been somewhat hampered by his surgeries, but the canine still listened to Dawson's commands.

"Are you ready to roll?" Sylvie asked, brushing crumbs from her jeans.

"Sure." He stood too, reaching for Diamond's reins. "How long will it take to get to the bottom?"

"An hour, maybe more," she answered.

He rubbed his sore abdomen, trying not to groan loud enough for her to hear him.

Sylvie took the lead. He had to smile at the image of her telling her husband to take a hike. It would take a strong man to handle her.

Not that he was vying for the chance. He preferred his life uncomplicated. Being a SEAL made having a relationship extremely difficult, but even now that he was out with his full pension, he was in no hurry to change his ways.

Maybe he was more like Sylvie than he wanted to admit.

She turned Fanny and headed down what he viewed as a treacherous trail. He kept one eye on Kilo and the other on Sylvie as they slowly descended the mountain.

He'd been home long enough to become accustomed to the altitude, but he still found himself feeling a bit breathless. Sylvie acted as if she were on a peaceful trail ride, swaying back and forth in the saddle like a natural.

He had to give her credit. The lady was one tough cowboy.

One of Diamond's hooves slipped on a rock. He gripped the gelding with his knees, and the animal quickly found his footing. Dawson breathed out a sigh of relief.

So far, Kilo was doing okay, but he still worried about the canine. This was one of the longest rides he'd taken the dog on, and he didn't want to harm the animal. Good thing Kilo was young enough to treat this like an exciting game. Every so often the yellow lab would lift his snout to sniff the air, no doubt taking in all the interesting scents surrounding them.

Hopefully, the slower pace would prevent the dog from getting too tired and worn out. There were other hazards too, like snakes and other varmints.

They were about halfway down the mountainside when Kilo abruptly began to growl. A second later, Dawson heard a rumbling noise. Turning in his saddle, his heart squeezed in his chest when he saw a large boulder bouncing down the side of the mountain, coming straight toward them.

"Sylvie! Look out!" He pulled back on the reins and jumped off Diamond. Bending at the waist, he grabbed Kilo. The trail was so narrow there wasn't much of an option to move the horse out of the way, but he did his best.

Holding Kilo to his chest, he plastered himself against the mountainside, hoping and praying the boulder would somehow miss them.

Made in United States
Troutdale, OR
04/07/2024

19011035R10135